# GERALD HAMMOND
## ADVERSE REPORT

By the same author:

# GERALD HAMMOND
# ADVERSE REPORT

St. Martin's Press
New York

Library of Congress Cataloging-in-Publication Data
Hammond, Gerald.
     Adverse report.
     I. Title.
PR6058.A55456A64   1989      823'.914      88-35642
ISBN 0-312-02858-X

First published in Great Britain by Macmillan London Limited.

First U.S. Edition

10 9 8 7 6 5 4 3 2 1

# GERALD HAMMOND
# ADVERSE REPORT

# ONE

If that letter, with its severe, legal letterhead and discouraging typeface, had reached me at any other time, I would probably have written back with instructions to sell immediately and to send me the money as soon as possible, and have put the whole thing out of my mind until the money arrived. After all, I had never known Uncle George well. One childhood visit hardly cements a relationship.

But London was roasting. The Azores high had stretched its hot hand northward to clasp Britain and most of Europe, and for once it was not pulling back like a nervous cat but was tightening its grip. Heat shimmered in the fuming streets. Even the parks were dry and dusty except for humid couples flopping on the grass. Everybody I knew had fled to somewhere cool, like the moon.

And I had broken with Stella. Or, rather, she had broken with me. Perhaps the heat had had more than a little to do with it. We had cohabited happily for a year or more, but life with a skinny, brown-haired and ginger-bearded writer already in his mid-thirties, modestly prolific but subsisting not far above the failure line, must have had few charms for a failed model and part-time swinger. As the heat arrived, so she had left.

I was surprised at how little I missed her, except at night. She had been out every day, chasing work and God alone knew what else, leaving me to my writing between bouts of trying to keep the house, or rather my grotty little flat, up to the standard which she imposed. Left to myself I had been free to let it revert towards the comfortable male slum which it had been before her arrival. But it was a hot, breathless, sweaty male slum and I loathed it.

Then came the letter, from an address in The Square, Newton Lauder.

Dear Mr Parbitter,

As you may know, your uncle, George Hatton, farmer, of Kirkton Mains Farm in East Lothian, died recently as the result of a tragic shooting accident.

He also owned Tansy House, near Newton Lauder, and bequeathed it to you by codicil to his last will. This is a small house, built of stone and slate late in the last century, and comprises a living room, kitchen, bathroom and three bedrooms (or two bedrooms and a study). The property also includes 50 acres of agricultural land which he was in the habit of letting. I append such further details as I have to hand.

Please let me know your intentions. If you wish me to dispose of the property on your behalf, I will do so. Otherwise, as your uncle's executor, I will proceed with the conveyance.

Yours sincerely,

Ralph Enterkin, WS.

The enclosures were a photograph of a house on a hill, backed by trees and looking pleasantly cool and fresh; and a page about such matters as Rateable Value and Feu Duty which I found slightly less comprehensible than the Dead Sea Scrolls.

I dabbed at the sweat on my face and upper chest, looked out of my window into some back gardens where a fat woman was reclining under a pink umbrella, and thought about it.

The lease on the flat would soon be up. For some time I had nursed a vague feeling that Town would be a good place to live outside. Not far out – Surrey perhaps or Kent – but far enough out that I could get to know my neighbours without depending on them for secondhand breath and petrol fumes. But Stella had been a town girl and a move had been out of the question during her time in residence, even if I could have afforded to compete with the civil servants and men of finance who had snapped up everything within commuting distance and beyond.

But . . . Scotland?

Perhaps, just as a summer retreat, if I could afford to keep it on.

No harm, I thought, in going to look. There was a roof and it would be cooler – if not bloody cold, as I remembered. The prospect of being bloody cold was perversely attractive. I had dim memories of paddling up a cold stream under trees and of walking on springy grass between huge rocks; of a mile of empty beach; of kind voices with an accent which had ever since struck a chord; of houses with tight railings, filled with the smell of baking and of unfamiliar polishes.

It would be a good time to go. I was bled dry of ideas and nobody seemed desperate to have me ghost an autobiography. My last format for a television series seemed to have gone plop into some bottomless pool, lost for ever.

Stella had wanted me to keep a car, some suitable symbol of status and mobility and masculinity. A car in London is only an expensive way of ensuring that you get plenty of exercise. But a motorbike can slip through traffic and be parked almost anywhere, and because the yobbos can identify with it they leave it alone. I got the Yamaha out of the shed behind Benny's store, packed the panniers and in the morning I was away.

Some of the heat was left behind in the city streets and, as the wind of my going blew the rest away, I wondered for the umpteenth time why, other than from habit, I stayed on in dear, horrid old London. To be near my agent? I saw him perhaps once a year. My various publishers preferred not to see me at all. To be near the big libraries? My small local library obtained any book I wanted. Museums, theatres, concert halls? I visited them rarely, if dragged. Stella had dragged me, but Stella was gone.

I could have made it in a day, by arriving after everything had closed. I imagined that Scotland was dead after the time for high tea. Derek Onslow, the oldest of my few friends, was a lecturer at Newcastle. I spent the evening with him and borrowed a bed for the night.

I seemed to have left the motorways behind. I rode on, sometimes through farmland and sometimes between heather-clad hills, half expecting to fall over the further edge. Less than an hour after crossing into Scotland I came across the sign for Newton Lauder.

It failed to surprise me. I had the usual belief of the non-Scot that Scotland comprised a few acres of heather surrounding Glasgow. If I had turned the pages of the road atlas I would have seen that Scotland continued north for as far as the distance from London to Land's End or Blackpool. The sign indicated, by means of a huge D-shape, that if I cared to accept the hospitality of Newton Lauder the same road would return me to the trunk route to Edinburgh and points north.

But it was Newton Lauder I wanted and, after a couple of miles through a valley of what I judged, ignorantly but correctly, to be good farmland, I came to a town of stone and slate, gardens on the road and trees looking over rooftops. An old town, small in scale, almost cosy, self-contained. The Square, which was really an elongated triangle, was dominated by the only tall modern building – the Town Hall, I assumed, wrongly. It housed the police and I was to become familiar with its interior.

I parked the bike among a row of others, some very expensive wheels among them, and stripped off my leathers while I looked around, tasting the atmosphere. The Square was ringed with shops, mostly the small, specialised shops which seemed to be disappearing in the South. And something was missing. Crowds. The kind of crowds which make your skull shrink would have been unthinkable there. Loving my fellow man only in small numbers, I felt the knots of years unwinding. The few people in sight were individuals. Their clothes were behind the times. I was dressed to melt into a Chelsea crowd, but here I would have stood out if there had been more than a few souls to stand out from.

The solicitor's brass plate was in a corner of The Square. I climbed a narrow stairway to where a dried-up old trout guarded an outer office. She looked at me over her half-glasses and sniffed. I had expected a solicitor in a small backwater to be available to clients but she seemed shocked at the very idea. Mr Enterkin, she said, had a client with him; and I could hear voices from the inner room, so this was not a ploy to impress me. She could fit me in, she said, 'at the back of two', unless I cared to wait? I am one of nature's non-waiters – I will not queue for the Second Coming and I said as much.

In the hotel there was a bar lunch within my means and the beer was surprisingly good. Some of the customers looked at me sidelong, curious rather than hostile.

8

A middle-aged local shared my table. He was fishing inside his suit and saw me looking at him. 'Lost my gallowsès,' he explained. I thought that he said 'glasses' – I was hardly to know that gallowses were braces – and told him that they were on his nose. He was vastly amused, once we had resolved our misunderstanding, and insisted on giving me a short course in Scots vocabulary.

I was back at the solicitor's office shortly after two.

Mr Enterkin, a fat little porker with a jovial expression and no discernible accent, received me in a room which would have been stark but for mounds of files and loose papers. He seemed prepared to chatter indefinitely, about my life and my recollections, faint as they were, of Uncle George and to reminisce about his own dealings with the deceased. I used the first break in his monologue to drag the conversation back to the subject of my legacy.

He looked at me reproachfully. 'Quite right,' he said. 'You mustn't let me ramble. You're here in good time.'

'I was glad of the excuse to come away,' I said. 'London's like an oven.'

'Very likely,' he said. 'But I was expecting a letter rather than an immediate visit.'

'You asked for instructions. Did you expect me to decide without seeing the place?'

His eyebrows, which made up at least a third of his total crop of hair, went up. 'You think you might keep it on? Well, time enough to decide. Where are you staying?'

I told him that I had made no arrangements. 'Could I occupy Tansy House?' I asked. 'Is it furnished?'

He paused and made a face while he thought about it and then he took a ring of keys out of a box-file. 'I see no reason why not,' he said. 'All the contents will come to you anyway.' He looked at his watch. 'I have another client due to descend on me shortly, but if you care to wait or to return I'll take you out and see you installed.'

I said that I would be quite capable of finding the place, given adequate directions.

'So be it. I should explain that the place is much as your uncle left it. He had been staying there for the few days immediately preceding his accident. I saw to it that any perishable food was

9

removed – it seemed prudent to switch the electricity off, which would have negated the functioning of the fridge and freezer – and I removed a shotgun, the partner to the one which he was using at the time of his death, and some papers which I deemed necessary for my purposes or for the continued running of the farm. Otherwise, nothing has been touched.'

From his letter, I had guessed that Tansy House had been kept for summer letting, but it seemed that I was wrong. 'You'd better tell me a bit more,' I said.

He snorted. 'I was endeavouring to do so when you cut me off,' he said stiffly. 'I will try to fill the gaps while being as terse as you seem to wish. You do know that he was one of a family of four – all now deceased? And that he never married? His main residence was the farm in East Lothian. He was a keen shot and he had friends in this area, so when he was left Tansy House by his widowed elder sister, Alice, he decided to retain it. He had previously been in the habit of seeking a bed from her, you see, whenever he had a shooting engagement hereabouts.' Here Mr Enterkin's manner began to show a certain embarrassment which I was not to understand until later. 'It became his habit to come here for – ah – for a break whenever time permitted, bringing with him the occasional – umm – guest, leaving the farm to be managed by his foreman under the occasional supervision of your cousin – who now inherits it.

'I acted as executor under his sister's will and that seemed to remind him to make a will of his own. In the will which I drew up he left everything, after a few minor bequests, to your cousin Alec, the only son of his brother John. Later, when he called to see me about a tenancy matter, he remarked that he had another nephew, Simon Parbitter, to wit yourself, living in London. The idea that one of his kin should be forced to reside in what he referred to as "The Great Wen" seemed to distress him.'

'Until this heatwave,' I said, 'I lived in London because I liked it.'

Mr Enterkin nodded solemnly. 'I explained to him that that was probably the case but he seemed unconvinced. Indeed, he must have been unable to believe that anyone would live in London from choice, because he modified his will. Unfortunately, he did so by codicil and without asking my advice, with the result that the codicil is worded with less than legal precision. It merely refers to the house and outbuildings "and all their contents".

'It could be argued – and frequently is argued – that "contents" are the furnishings pertaining to the house itself and not the owner's personal trivia. But in my view the words "and all their contents", coupled with the lack of any mention of personal trivia elsewhere in the will, suggested that the testator intended you to have everything which was in the house at the time of his death. I put the point to your cousin and he agreed, and in writing. So the matter is settled.'

'Nice of him,' I said.

'Indeed. Although I did point out that if he wished to dispute my interpretation I would feel it my duty, in fairness to the other beneficiary – yourself – to reconsider such questions as the proper ownership of your uncle's Land-Rover, which would have been a content of one of the outbuildings had he not taken it with him to his death. He may also have been motivated by a disinclination to be saddled with clearing out another house, in addition to Kirkton Mains Farm. Your uncle was not in the habit of discarding anything for which a use might be found.'

'I suppose I could hire somebody to clear the place out,' I said. 'Or call in a junk dealer.'

His eyebrows shot up again. 'I should have a care,' he said. 'Your cousin may not have realised the value of some of your uncle's possessions.'

'Such as?'

'Such as a set of ivory-backed hairbrushes. Such as gold studs, cufflinks and watchchain. A very good wristwatch by Harrison, which he never wore when shooting in case the jolt of recoil should damage its mechanism. And a shotgun which, I am assured, is of some value, despite the fact that its twin seems to have caused his death.'

'I only know what was in your letter,' I said. 'What did happen?'

He shrugged. 'I know little more myself. No doubt we shall hear the facts tomorrow.'

'Tomorrow?'

He stared at me. 'Naturally I had supposed that your

11

precipitate arrival was because of the Fatal Accident Enquiry tomorrow. I assumed that you must have heard or even, conceivably, been called; but apparently not. In normal course, the funeral will follow a few days later. I shall, of course, attend the Fatal Accident Enquiry. And you?'

'An inquest, do you mean?' I asked.

'We do not have coroners' inquests in Scotland. Just an enquiry in front of the sheriff, if the procurator fiscal deems it necessary.'

The enquiry itself would no doubt be reported, and I could see little benefit in learning the facts a few hours earlier. On the other hand, a writer must always be absorbing backgrounds and local colour. 'I'll be there,' I said. 'Where is it?'

'Linlithgow, that being the sheriffdom where it happened. You have a car?'

'I've a motorbike.'

He clicked his tongue. 'You must let me give you a lift. I'll call for you at eight.' I blinked at that and he nodded sympathetically. 'I know,' he said. 'A damnable hour, but we'll have a long road before us. One of the witnesses will be with us. And, if you'll forgive my mentioning it, I would suggest something a little less exotic in the way of clothing. Perhaps one of your uncle's suits? You look to have been much of a size . . .'

We had no time for more. His next client arrived and seemed to take precedence, although, from the glimpse I had of him in the outer office, he was no more than an elderly scarecrow in a worn-out kilt. Which, come to think of it, was the first kilt I had seen around Newton Lauder.

The solicitor's directions turned out to be both clear and accurate. I left the town on a road that climbed the eastern side of the valley past a small hospital, crossed a ridge draped with moorland in full flower and descended again into farmland. There, shortly beyond the crest and within three or four miles of the town, I found Tansy House, perched on a slight rise and facing south across the road from which it was separated only by a narrow strip of rockery.

The photographs had shown little but the rather prim and self-satisfied-looking two-up, four-down, neither a cottage nor a mansion. Illogically, I had envisaged neighbours and a street scene. The solitude caught me unprepared until I saw that the fields which stretched to the next line of hills were dotted with farmhouses. Behind the house, beyond a surprisingly well-kept walled garden and a small field, rose a tall wood. There was a recent concrete garage where the Yamaha would be safe and sheltered.

The house, when I managed to find the right key among several others, had the derelict smell peculiar to houses which have stood unventilated in hot weather, overlying a comfortable scent of old pipe tobacco. I did a tour, opening the sash-and-case windows as I went. Tansy House seemed to have been furnished many years before in a style which was comfortable and nothing more – neither modern nor antique, not art deco or anything else – and to have remained unchanged except for the addition of a television set and an inexpensive music centre. It was hardly spacious, but it was several times the size of my London flat.

I had no time for detailed examination. A least the place seemed dry. I emptied my panniers by dumping my clothes onto my uncle's bed, rode back into Newton Lauder and went shopping in a small supermarket where they seemed to find my accent as funny as I found theirs.

The solicitor had said something about having the meters read. I had expected this to take the three weeks which it would have taken at home, but either he had some clout or the Scots react with special promptitude to the idea of somebody getting electricity on somebody else's account, because the meter reader was at the door when I got back. He was a garrulous little chap with more than his share of what I was coming to recognise as the local accent, but at least he turned the electricity on for me and saw that everything was working. He said that my uncle had been well liked in the neighbourhood despite the rarity of his visits. When I mentioned the – umm – guests to which the solicitor had referred, he changed the subject.

When he was gone, no doubt to spread a great deal of inaccurate gossip about me, I got down to clearing a living space for myself and airing fresh sheets. As I headed for my uncle's bed that night, earlier than would have been my habit in London, lights were springing up at unexpected points as hidden cottages revealed their presence.

13

I wondered idly whether I could ever settle down in such a place. I decided that I would hate to live so close to a busy road and then, just before I dropped into a deep sleep, laughed at myself because, apart from my motorbike and the meter reader's van, the total of traffic past the house since my arrival had been one tractor, one car and a young girl on a pony. The car had slowed until I thought that the driver intended to pay a visit, but when I switched on a light the car had spurted angrily away.

# TWO

The telephone at least had not been disconnected. Mr Enterkin, apparently, had not feared that the mice would offset the loneliness of the empty house by calling their relatives in far-off lands. A morning call had me up and ready by the time a car's horn sounded outside.

The solicitor seemed to look at me with less disapproval than he had shown the day before. I still saw nothing wrong with my own wardrobe; but among my uncle's suits I had found one, in pale grey flannel, which fitted me well and was cut in a style which was returning to fashion. With it, I wore a shirt of my own and one of my uncle's ties.

'I did not know,' Enterkin said in greeting, 'that you were a member of the Scottish Nationalist Party.'

'The tie?'

'Yes. But never mind. You are in some good company, some less so. This is Keith Calder.'

Calder shook hands from his position at the wheel of an old but well-preserved Rover. He was into his forties and almost out of them again, but his Mediterranean style of good looks (perhaps a legacy from one of the many Spanish sailors wrecked on the Scottish coast after the Armada) were wearing well and his black hair showed no more than a distinguished trace of grey at the temples to attest that the colour was original. His manner was gloomy, showing no sign of the mischievous humour with which I was to be poked and prodded later. Enterkin took the other front seat and I was relegated to the rear.

The car, I gathered, was Enterkin's ewe lamb and he seemed irritated that Calder had insisted on driving, but Calder remained firm. 'If you drive, Ralph, we might get there by the right time,

15

but tomorrow. I'll get us there with time in hand for a coffee.'

Enterkin sighed deeply. 'Try to leave some tread on my tyres,' he said, 'and remember that the man in the driver's seat pays for the petrol.'

'Sue me,' Calder said. I hoped that it was the comfortable bickering, quite without trace of malice, which can become habitual between two old friends. Over Calder's shoulder I saw that the tank was half-full. He was a good driver but the solicitor caught his breath whenever a bend or another vehicle was in sight.

We slipped through Newton Lauder and headed north. To my eyes, accustomed to the ribbon developments of the South or the confining unreality of motorways, the sight of such endless tracts of open countryside was almost agoraphobic. After an hour or so we were skirting a city which I identified from the signposts as Edinburgh.

By way of making polite conversation, the solicitor asked some question about my writing activities. Calder, who seemed to have other things on his mind and to regard my presence as an irrelevancy, pricked up his ears. 'Are you Simon Parbitter, the mystery writer?' he asked.

'Among other work,' I admitted. My crime-writing, fact and fiction, together with the ghosted autobiographies, accounted for most of my income; but I would rather be remembered for my carefully researched political histories or my two historical novels.

'I don't have much time to read fiction,' he said. (I wondered how many before him had used those words to me.) 'My wife and daughter read it by the hour. They've shown me pieces from your books.'

'Oh?' I said. I prepared to sound modestly flattered, but he fell silent and concentrated on his driving and whatever was worrying him.

Signposts indicated Glasgow, but instead of the Glasgow motorway we took one posted for Stirling. Scotland seemed to go on for ever. (I realised later that we had still penetrated only a third of its length.) We came off the motorway for Linlithgow, which turned out to be an even older town than Newton Lauder and somewhat larger. As promised, we had time to visit a neat café for coffee over which Enterkin rambled on about Linlithgow's long history.

16

I was becoming absorbed in his discourse when Calder suddenly came out of his trance and scowled at me. 'Luger revolvers!' he said.

'I beg your pardon?'

'*The Spinet Legacy*. You had somebody rushing around brandishing a Luger revolver.'

I felt my ears go hot. 'Is there something wrong with that?'

'Aye. The Luger, or Parabellum, was a design of semi-automatic or self-loading pistol which you'd probably call an automatic. In fact, it was an improvement on the original Borchardt. There never was a Luger revolver yet. And you had another character checking the magazine of his revolver!'

Enterkin chuckled. 'Perhaps I should have warned you that Keith's a gunsmith with a special interest in history.'

'I hardly think,' I said stiffly, 'that the average reader would know the difference.'

'The less your reader knows, the greater your obligation to instruct him. In *Scare*, you made it clear that the baddy was carrying a double-barrel hammerless shotgun. And then you wrote, "I heard the click as he cocked the actuating mechanism". What in hell was that supposed to mean?'

'Exactly what it said.'

'It didn't mean a damn thing,' he grunted. He got up to visit the toilet.

'Is he always as rude as that?' I asked.

'Just sometimes,' Enterkin said. He seemed to be highly amused at my expense. 'Don't take him amiss. He's trying to be helpful, in his way. Ask his advice tomorrow and he'll go to endless trouble to help you. Just now, he's worried about this case. You'll hear what it's about later. I don't understand the half of it myself, but the depute fiscal's had her knife into Keith ever since he gave evidence here last year. He turned the prosecution's case on its ear and the lady ended up with egg all over her unlovely face. She's not the kind of person to take kindly to such treatment and this may be her chance to get even.'

I felt more cheerful as we walked to the Sheriff Court building. It seemed that my harshest critic faced harassment in his turn.

Calder was diverted into a witness room but Enterkin and I took seats in the small courtroom. Among the scattering of onlookers I identified a couple of bored reporters by their notebooks. Just behind them was sitting a stocky man of about my own age, with hair like a coir doormat and a weatherbeaten face, whose cast of features was vaguely familiar. I decided that he probably resembled some actor and forgot him for the moment.

The sheriff was disposing of the previous case – rather severely, I thought, although it was difficult to judge without knowing all the facts. ('Sheriff Dougall,' Enterkin whispered. 'Intransigent old beggar!') The sheriff's voice was noticeably patrician and yet undoubtedly Scottish, which gave me an uneasy feeling because I had supposed, in my innocence, that the upper strata of the Law were above provincialism.

Apart from the lack of a jury and the addressing of the sheriff as My Lord, the case, when it came on, could have been taken for an English inquest.

The depute procurator fiscal, a stout lady nearing middle age and blessed with the most ferocious jaw-line I had ever seen, introduced the broad facts in terms so short as to be worthless and then called her first witness. This was a police officer who had been called to Knoweheid Farm near Howeburn. ('Hilltop Farm,' Enterkin whispered in explanation.) There, among the whins ('Gorse') he had been shown the body of a man. This was later identified as the body of George Hatton. The head and hands were badly damaged and the remains of a shotgun were nearby.

After formal evidence of identification had been given and accepted, a pathologist testified that death had been instantaneous and had resulted from 'damage to the head apparently caused by an explosion and the consequent intrusion of metal fragments, portions of some firearm'. The deceased had been in good health and there were no traces of drugs or alcohol. The right collarbone had been fractured and the hands badly damaged by the same explosion. All the injuries were consistent with having been caused by a bursting shotgun.

The proceedings, which until then had been about as lively as a reading from the 'phone-book, came to life when Hector Duffus was called. Mr Duffus, who was a farmer and the occupier of Knoweheid Farm, was a gnarled old man in his seventies but for all his years he radiated health and vitality. His accent was strong and his speech was threaded with Scots words and phrases of which, to my relief, the sheriff himself frequently asked the meaning. Apart from mentioning that he caused a ripple of amusement with the phrase 'a fiddler's bidding', which turned out to mean a last-minute invitation, I will make no attempt to reproduce the rich texture of his dialect.

According to Mr Duffus, the four who had made up the shooting party had shot together for many seasons, exchanging invitations every winter and occasionally meeting for a rabbit-shoot during the summer whenever the rabbit population merited an assault. This occasion had been suggested by an explosion of rabbits on Knoweheid Farm and he had taken advantage of the quiet spell which often precedes the harvest to invite his three nearer friends for a day combining sport and control. Because of the distance involved and the mundane nature of the event he had not mentioned it to George Hatton until one of the original invitees had been forced to drop out, but my uncle had accepted the 'fiddler's bidding' with enthusiasm.

At this point, the depute fiscal had to discourage Duffus from expounding at length on the damage which the rabbits had been causing to his crops.

At first, Duffus continued, all had gone to plan. The dogs had hunted well and there had been a substantial cull. After an hour or so they had come to a knoll. My uncle had gone to stand guard over a small gulley which formed a favourite escape-route to holes near the top of the knoll, while the others put dogs through the gorse which ringed the base. A few shots had been fired. Suddenly, they had heard a loud report ('a wappin' fuff'). After a short hesitation, because shots can seem to vary greatly in loudness according to the angle at which they are fired relative to the hearer, he had walked up the gulley and found his friend lying exactly as the police had seen him. He had sent for the police and an ambulance immediately and the day's sport had been abandoned.

The next witness, one Duncan Cameron of Shotsports (Edinburgh) Ltd, took up a disproportionate amount of the court's time extolling his own experience and expertise as a specialist in firearms, with special reference to the number of reports written and the weight of evidence given. Even to my inexperienced ear the qualifications sounded thin, but he gave his evidence with the self-important pomposity which often impresses the gullible. His accent I thought precious.

He had examined the pieces of firearm which were before the court, he said. They were the remains of a double-barrel, twelve-bore, semi-hammerless shotgun, built to the design and patent of David Bentley by Roper of Sheffield. It had been a gun of quality in its day but it had burst in use with quite exceptional violence.

The depute procurator fiscal asked him whether he could offer any reason for the burst.

Mr Cameron smirked. 'I can indeed,' he said. 'I examined with some care the remains of the barrels and of the cartridges which had been in the chambers. One cartridge had been almost totally destroyed, but I could discern that the other had been loaded with a modern propellant powder, one of the proprietary mixtures now available and based on nitrocellulose. However, the proofmarks on the flats of the breeches could still be made out and it was clear that the gun had been proved for black powder only.'

The sheriff leaned forward, God condescending to speak to a mortal. 'In this context, what is meant by "proof"?' I had the impression that he knew the answer and that his question was only for the record.

Cameron was evidently delighted by the invitation to further pontification. 'In Britain,' he said, 'there is a legal requirement that no firearm may be sold unless it has been proved at either the London or Birmingham Proof House or at an overseas establishment of equivalent status. The procedures include the firing through each barrel of a cartridge generating pressures substantially greater than those to be expected in normal use.'

'And black powder?'

Cameron smiled and nodded. His tone and manner suggested that only he and the sheriff were capable of appreciating the finer points of his evidence. 'At the time the gun was built, my lord, black powder, also known as gunpowder, was the normal propellant. That powder generates lower pressures than the modern nitro or smokeless powders. I can therefore state that the deceased was using cartridges which produced pressures as great as or greater than that of the proof cartridges with which the gun had been tested nearly a hundred years ago.'

'I see,' said the sheriff. He began writing, as if, for him, the matter was over.

The depute procurator fiscal looked down at her papers. 'Of what were the gun-barrels constructed?' she asked. It struck me as an odd question.

'They were of the so-called "Damascus" construction; that is to say, they were made from a fine weave of iron and steel, wound around a mandrel and hammer-welded. That construction was erroneously believed to produce very strong barrels. It fell into disuse as soon as the techniques of modern steelmaking were developed.'

'Would these factors be sufficient to explain the tragedy?'

Cameron smiled loftily. 'These matters are hardly susceptible to mathematical calculation,' he said. 'Any further evidence has literally gone up in smoke.' He paused for effect and there was a faint whisper of amusement. 'But it must be said that if a barrel which had presumably been discharging similar cartridges for some years chose that occasion to burst with such extreme violence, it suggests that the cartridge may have been faulty. Loading errors can sometimes produce pressures many times the norm.'

As Cameron bowed and left the courtroom, I found myself agreeing with the sheriff. Why we had brought Calder along seemed to be the only mystery remaining.

Calder was the next and final witness. As he entered, he saw the shattered gun which lay on the central table and checked in his stride for a moment. While he took the oath, his eyes were still fixed in that direction. His examination is worth recording in full.

'Tell the court your name.'

'Keith Calder.'

'And your occupation?'

'Gunsmith . . .'

'Thank you . . .'

'. . . gun dealer and . . .'

'Thank you very much.' The depute fiscal's voice drowned him out. 'Please tell the court your place of business.'

'I am the proprietor of the gunshop in Newton Lauder. And I may say that I . . .'

It was the sheriff's turn to interrupt. 'Is it your intention to qualify Mr Calder as an expert witness?' he asked.

21

'No, my lord, it is not.'

Calder remained calm, but I could see that it cost him an effort. 'My lord,' he said, 'I was only attempting to answer the question.'

'Please confine yourself to doing that and no more.' The sheriff nodded to the depute fiscal.

'You were acquainted with the late Mr Hatton?'

'I was. Principally as my customer, but I had met him socially.'

She picked up a – to me – unrecognisable lump of metal. 'This has been identified as a part of the gun which burst, killing him. It bears a number. Can you confirm that it was in fact his gun?'

Calder studied the part for a few seconds and I could see that his mind was in overdrive. 'It was,' he said. 'One of a pair.'

'Did you ever carry out any work on this gun?'

'I did.'

'Please tell the court what it was.'

'I don't know which gun of the pair that is,' Calder said. 'If . . .'

'Then how do you know that you carried out work on it?' the depute fiscal snapped.

'Because I did work on both of them.'

His lordship was frowning. 'Is all this really relevant?'

'As it transpires, m'lud, no. I only wished to show that the gun had been through Mr Calder's hands. Mr Calder, what was the proof status of the guns?'

'Each gun had been proved for black powder and was still within the requirements for that proof.'

'You knew that the guns were only proved for gunpowder? Yet you returned them to him for use with smokeless cartridges?'

'They were his guns. They were in proof.'

'But for black powder only.'

Calder bit back a sharp answer and took several deep breaths. 'The law does not make a distinction,' he said carefully. 'It's hard to see how it could, while reproduction guns are still being made for black powder shooting. I warned Mr Hatton, several times, that he should send his guns for nitro proof, or use black powder cartridges only, or retire them. I had no power to do more. If I had retained his guns and he had come to this court, his lordship would . . .'

'His lordship knows better than you do what his decision would have been,' the depute fiscal said quickly. 'I now hand you the remains of the cartridges out of the gun. What can you tell me about them?'

Calder picked up a damaged but recognisable yellow cartridge. 'This appears to have been a standard cartridge from the Huddersfield Cartridge Company. From the printing, it was sold through my shop. Not enough of the other cartridge is left for the printing to be seen, but the base, though totally flattened, seems to have been similar.'

'They would have been loaded with modern nitrocellulose powder?'

'As originally sold, yes. They could have been reloaded. The owner of a black powder gun will often load new or used cases using gunpowder.'

From a case beneath her table the depute fiscal produced a cartridge belt. About half of the pockets were empty, the others containing a dozen or so cartridges. 'I show you the belt which the deceased was wearing. You would agree that the remaining cartridges all bear the imprint of your shop?'

'Yes.'

'And show no signs of having been reloaded?'

Calder studied them carefully. 'True,' he said.

At that moment I realised that his apprehension had been justified. The lady was gunning for him, or why had she taken so much trouble with her homework?

'So,' she said, 'knowing that Mr Hatton's guns were proved only for black powder, you sold him modern cartridges loaded with smokeless nitro powder?'

Calder was looking as black as the gunpowder under discussion and about as explosive, but he still held himself from bursting. 'That does not necessarily follow,' he said. 'I spoke very seriously to Mr Hatton about the dangers. I even hand-loaded some cartridges with black powder for him to use and to satisfy himself that he was losing little or nothing in performance. After that, if he ran short of cartridges while in residence at Newton Lauder, he might well have preferred to have somebody else buy them for him. I certainly don't remember selling him any. But even if I had done so, I would not have been contravening the law. There are many such guns in use, and mishaps are rare.'

'But they do happen?'

'They do.' Calder paused and then plunged on. 'But I'll tell you this: such bursts as I've seen in similar guns have been minor affairs. Often, only the first twist of the Damascus barrel is sprung out. The user gets a fright and loses his eyebrows, maybe even a little skin. I have never, ever, seen a gun destroyed like that one, nor anything like it.'

The sheriff stirred again and looked at the depute procurator fiscal. 'You still have not qualified Mr Calder as an expert witness,' he said.

'I was not giving an opinion, my lord,' Calder said. 'I was stating facts within my own experience.'

His lordship ignored him and spoke to the depute fiscal. 'I have no wish to hurry you,' he said, 'but do please bear in mind that the hour of adjournment is almost upon us and we have another case called for this afternoon.'

The depute fiscal swung back to Calder. I could not see her face but I could hear the triumph in her voice. 'Briefly, then, Mr Calder, you're suggesting, from your experience, that not only was Mr Hatton using cartridges emanating from your shop which were unsuited to his gun but, in addition, that the fatal cartridge must in some way have been exceptional or faulty?'

Calder hesitated again. 'You would have to put that question to the Huddersfield Cartridge Company,' he said.

'Thank you, Mr Calder. That will be all.'

A few minutes later the sheriff was giving his decision, that my uncle had died by misadventure. In summing up the facts he managed to imply, without quite stating, that Keith Calder had been careless if not downright negligent.

The gunsmith was fizzling with fury as we left the room.

# THREE

I only half-listened to Calder's hissing plaint. The stocky man with hair like a coconut mat broke away from a group which included the witness Duffus and caught me by the sleeve as I walked by. 'It is Simon Parbitter?' he said. 'I'm Alec Hatton. Your cousin.'

So that was why he had seemed familiar. I shook his hand. 'It must be twenty years,' I said.

'Nearer thirty. I suppose we've both changed.'

'We'd be oddities if we hadn't,' I pointed out.

'That's true.' He paused to look at his watch. His clothes, I noticed, were off the peg, heavy and serviceable, not new but well kept. 'I wanted to talk to you, but I'm with Uncle George's shooting pals and we're just going to lunch. Join us?'

'I'd like to,' I said. 'But I'm with . . .'

He looked round. Enterkin and Calder had stopped a few yards away. Alec nodded a greeting. 'I don't think our uncle's solicitor or his gunsmith would be out of place,' he said. 'Shall we all join up and hold a mini-wake?'

Enterkin seemed to have doubts but Calder was keen. 'Strame House?' he suggested.

'We'll see you there, then.'

The others moved off but Calder turned to the solicitor. 'The law's finished with those bits of gun, hasn't it?'

'Apparently so.'

'Ralph, as the deceased's executor,' Calder said urgently, 'could you claim those bits before they get dumped in the bucket or somebody else thinks of grabbing them?'

'I could. But . . .'

'Let's not argue, let's do it.'

25

The solicitor threw up his hands and went back into the courtroom, muttering to himself.

'I'm not happy about this,' Calder said. 'There's something not right.'

'It's no skin off your nose,' I said. 'He was my uncle, not yours.'

'Then you should be even less happy than I am. Hang on a moment, there goes the pathologist. I met him in the witness room. A useful lad. Gabbie.' He darted off, leaving me to kick my heels in the empty corridor. 'Gabbie', I had learned from my friend in the hotel, meant talkative.

In two minutes, he was back. 'The pathologist tells me that there was no shot in your uncle,' he said. 'Damn!'

I gaped at him. 'Why would there have been?' I asked.

'Think about it. That bloody woman set me up,' he added indignantly. 'You wait and see what the papers make of it tomorrow.'

'I don't suppose they'll print more than the bare verdict,' I said.

He humphed. 'Cameron'll make sure they do. He hates my guts.'

This seemed to be going a bit far. 'To the extent of telling lies?'

'There's lies and lies. He's probably convinced himself that he's right and I'm wrong.'

Enterkin returned with a paper sack which rattled. We walked to the car. He dropped the sack into the boot and took the driver's seat. I was relegated once more to the rear. I could see why Calder had insisted on taking the wheel that morning. The solicitor drove very slowly and yet gave the impression of being quite out of touch with his car. It was as if he expected it at any moment to take the initiative from him, perhaps by sprouting legs or wings.

Calder spoke over his shoulder to me. 'At lunch, find out what you can. Your uncle's life-style, his last few days, that sort of thing. If I ask all the questions, it'll look too obvious. Don't let on that we know anything's wrong.'

'Do we really know that something's wrong?'

'No, we don't. We have a verdict,' Enterkin pointed out.

'Not necessarily a correct one,' Calder said.

'As far as the law is concerned, the facts are contained in the verdict.'

'And if those facts happen to be wrong,' Calder said, 'would you, as his executor, still want to proceed? For God's sake, don't slow down any more,' he added as Enterkin took his foot off the accelerator, 'or they'll be serving dinner by the time we get there. Look at it this way. If the sheriff was misadvised, which he was, it's not out of the question that one of the beneficiaries arranged for death. Would you want to go ahead and distribute their legacies in those circumstances?'

'Well, thank you very much,' I said. 'I hadn't been out of London for six weeks until the day before yesterday and I haven't been in Scotland since I was a boy.'

Enterkin met my eye in the driving mirror but said nothing. We drove for a mile in irritable silence. Enterkin nerved himself and overtook a tractor and trailer. 'H'm,' he said. As a comment, I found it lacking in precision.

Another subject seemed overdue. 'What did you do to Cameron to get up his nose like that?' I asked Calder.

The solicitor chuckled and the gunsmith gave a small snort of amusement. 'There's a disreputable little gun-dealer called Moray. Christian name Abraham, if that can ever be called Christian. He sold a gun and the purchaser showed it to Duncan Cameron, who smelt a rat and ran to the procurator fiscal with it. That . . . that unfeminine female prosecuted and called Cameron as a witness. Unfortunately for them, Ralph here, who was for the defence, consulted me. Abe Moray certainly deserved to be put away – but not for that particular sin, of which he was quite guiltless.

'The gun had originally been built undersized and proved for gunpowder as a thirteen-bore. They used to do that sometimes, to allow a margin for lapping out the pitting which was common with the corrosive primers they used in those days. Then, around the turn of the century, it had been re-proved for nitro as a twelve-bore. Cameron and the Beastess with the Leastest tried to convince the sheriff – not Dougall, it was the other one sitting that day – that Abe had falsified the proof-marks, largely on the grounds that the Proof House stamp looked slightly different from the usual run.

'My wife, who's a photography nut, went chasing around the country photographing proof-marks, and we came up with half a dozen which matched the other exactly, and on guns which

Abe had never been within a mile of. The Proof House had been using several different punches, that was all. It would hardly have made a ripple except that Cameron, conceited slob that he is, had tipped off some friendly reporters that he was going to be sensational, and the reporters turned out not to be so friendly after all. It did his reputation a lot of no good.'

'And that's the understatement of the year,' Enterkin said. 'From what I heard, his customers got nervous about being landed in losing court-cases. Word goes round.'

'That's what I'm afraid of,' Calder said. 'Word going round. I don't want to be thought of as a muck-stirrer.'

'No doubt,' Enterkin said, 'you would prefer that the more recent purchasers from your stock of antique guns were not encouraged to look too closely at them.'

'Say that outside this car,' Calder growled, 'and I'll find another solicitor and sue you. Privilege only stretches so far.'

Strame House Hotel, when we came to it, was a gracious old building which had been extended in a modern but sympathetic style. It looked strangely opulent to my eyes, being set in wide gardens in open country instead of hemmed by houses.

My cousin, together with our uncle's shooting friends, was already at a table in a svelte lounge-bar and I found a large glass of whisky in my hand before he had completed the introductions.

Where I had lived for most of my life the gender roles are becoming softer-edged, so I was not as surprised as I might have been to realise that a woman had been among the guns. Mrs Emily Grant was tall, past forty and severely dressed. I could imagine her handling a gun with ruthless efficiency and yet she was one of those women who manage to look feminine and even sexy despite age and every self-made obstacle. In part, this was due to a rich figure and large, bright eyes, but it was enhanced by a voice which was low for a woman's but soft and insinuating. I thought that a man could go to bed with that voice and never mind the body, firm though that still was. I gathered that she had been a widow for some years, inheriting both a farm and a place among the men from her late husband, and that she ran her farm with the aid of a manager.

The other two men, Jim Fergus and Neil McDonald, were near neighbours to each other. Although not as old as Hector Duffus,

Fergus resembled him in that nobody could have taken either of them for anything but what they were, Scottish farmers too long rooted in the land ever to be transplanted.

Neil McDonald, introduced simply as 'the builder', was a large man, just as broadly spoken but without that patient calm which farmers learn. He chain-smoked, so that his hands and even his chin were stained yellow. One of his arms was in a sling – the result, he explained, of a fall from scaffolding. It was he who had cried off from the shooting party.

Another huge whisky appeared while I was still trying to get everyone straight. I muttered vague thanks in the hope that they would fetch up with whoever had bought the round, and turned to my cousin who was on my left. 'Where do you live these days?' I asked.

'Edinburgh, until this week.' He looked at me shyly, as if about to reveal some delicate secret. 'But I'm moving out to Kirkton Mains Farm, anticipating the settlement of the estate. The farm has to be managed.'

'Fair enough,' I said. 'I've moved into Tansy House. You fancy the rural life, do you?'

He blinked but nodded and his face took on the faraway look of the Buddhist nearing nirvana. 'I acted as Uncle George's manager for years, off and on, whenever he wanted a break,' he said. 'The place has become part of me. I graduated from agricultural college, but there was never the capital to set me up. I've been selling farm machinery for yonks but I'd have given both arms and a leg for a crack at the real thing.'

'And now you don't have to,' I said. Here at least was one person with a motive to put Uncle George under the ground. But would he have talked so openly if he had done so? Thinking it over, I decided that he would unless he were a fool – which he was not. Naïve, perhaps. The cunning looks which I would have expected of a machinery salesman were lacking, unless that blandness was itself a subtle disguise. Even after the sheriff's verdict, to have pretended a lie might have invited suspicion. 'Did you know that the farm was coming your way?'

'He told me last year, but I never expected ... I thought that he'd have at least twenty years to go. Of course, I'll have to sell off some land to capitalise it, but twelve-fifty acres is a bit unwieldy for a small farm. Either too big or too small. Trouble is, it's a rotten time to sell land.'

'Why?' I asked. He could apply the question to whatever he liked.

'Two pissing wet summers in a row,' he explained. 'Farmers with well-drained, sandy soil got away with it. Anybody on clay was doomed. Most arable farms are loaded with debt for the next few years . . .'

'Not Uncle George?'

'Thank God, no! He was too good a farmer and too thrifty. Even so, he was almost into the red and the place needs re-stocking and some new machinery. *He* could have borrowed – the banks are extending loans to prop up the price of land rather than lose their security – but I'm a newcomer as far as the banks are concerned.' He sighed and made a polite effort to forget his own troubles. 'Of course,' he said, 'I've been able to keep track of you more easily than you could of me. The flyleaves of your book jackets kept me up to date. I liked the historical novels.'

'Thanks,' I said. I was glad that the talk had left agriculture, which bored me, but I always found it difficult to respond to comments about my books.

Calder had been sitting quietly, taking in the talk of the two farming men about the chances of barley going for malting, whatever that might mean, and to the advice which Enterkin was giving to Mrs Grant about how to make her will; but he must have caught Alec's last remark. 'Gatling gun,' he said suddenly.

I said, 'What?'

'Gatling gun,' he repeated. 'You had the Union army using Gatling machine-guns during the Civil War. You weren't far out. Gatling had designed it in the first year of the war, but the Union army didn't adopt it until eighteen sixty-six, the year after it ended.'

'I'm terribly, terribly sorry,' I said, and turned back to my cousin.

Alec was grinning. 'I enjoyed it anyway,' he said.

I was half-way down my second drink. I had never been very fond of whisky, but this was something different and I said so.

'A double malt, laddie,' Duffus said, 'and fifteen years old.'

'I could learn to like it.'

'With perseverance,' Enterkin said, 'you might even learn to appreciate it. Bring it with you. Our table's ready.'

We moved into a dining room which was expensively under-stated, muted in colour and sound, hygienic without the use of plastics. It was the kind of place to which I could imagine rich men taking girls out from London and telling them to ignore the prices down the margin of the menu just to be sure that they would look and be impressed. I looked and was frankly terrified. I hoped that I was somebody's guest. If local custom decreed that the heir picked up the bill on such occasions, then surely my cousin. . . .

After we had ordered, one of those sudden silences came down like a great fleecy-lined candle-snuffer. More to break it than to please Calder I said, 'I hadn't seen my uncle since I was a child. How old was he?'

Old Hector Duffus grinned maliciously. 'I doubt he'd changed much in the last few years,' he said. 'He was sixty-two.'

'An' fitter than some as were half his age,' Jim Fergus said.

I pretended not to notice that I was being subtly needled. Let the two old boys poke their oblique Caledonian fun at the foreigner if it gave them pleasure. 'Tell me about him,' I said to nobody in particular. 'You must all have known him well.'

For some reason there was a faint stir of amusement. 'Some better than others,' McDonald said. 'See, now. He was a lifelong bachelor. Grand company and he could tell a good tale when he wanted. He liked his drappie . . .' McDonald saw that I was puzzled and indicated his glass '. . . but never let it get in the way of business. Got banned from driving once, for two years. But that's happened to better men.'

'I'm banned for life,' Jim Fergus said with quiet pride. Clearly he considered himself to be among them.

'He was a great hand at stick-making and wi' the pipes forbye,' Duffus said. 'And a first-class shot. He used to win medals, using that same pair of guns.'

There was a momentary silence.

'Did he hit his rabbit with that last shot?' Calder asked. 'I've been surprised how often a man with a burst barrel insists that his last shot killed the quarry.'

Duffus looked at the others and then shrugged. 'That I

31

couldn't tell you,' he said. 'There was a dead rabbit nearby, but I've no way of knowing whether it was that shot or another. We left it lying. It seemed to be a part of the mishanter, so to speak. Another yin came bolting out of the gulley.'

McDonald grunted. 'I'm no' a farmer mysel',' he said, 'but I jalouse he was an able one. Would I be right?'

The farmers, two men and the widow, nodded in unison. 'A canny man,' Duffus said, 'and aye kenned whit way the market would gang next.'

'But for the two bad years,' Mrs Grant said, 'he'd have died a wealthy man.'

'But he didn't,' I said.

'As to that,' said Enterkin, 'I can't comment. The estate will be published in due course.'

Jim Fergus glanced at him in amusement. 'Even if there was a few bills unpaid,' he said, 'Dod would've been wellgathered. Tak' his land at – what? – echt hunnert the acre?'

'Quite that,' Duffus said, 'even now.'

'Then there's the house and steadings, machinery, stock and standing crops . . . Did he own his combine or was it leased?'

'Bought it cash,' Duffus said. 'I was wi' him when he wrote the cheque. The mannie at the bank near messed his breeks over it.'

Fergus nodded slowly. 'A braw penny there,' he said. 'I'd say, all told, no' much short of a million and a half.'

Alec was avoiding my eye.

Our meal arrived then and the conversation drifted off into the prospects for the imminent harvest. The consensus seemed to be that a day's rain would do no harm but that the fine weather, if it held, had come, for once, at the right time.

One point was nagging at me. 'Losing his licence must have made life difficult for a farmer,' I said. 'How did he manage?'

The conversation hiccuped for a moment – hung fire, I supposed that Calder would have said.

'You learn to get by,' Fergus said.

'He managed very well,' Mrs Grant said firmly, 'even if he didn't have a daughter on call. He could use the Land-Rover on his own farm and nobody could say boo to him. At other times, I drove him. I'm little more than a sort of secretary on my farm, so I could spare the time. And it gave me the use of his Ford.' At that moment, regrettably, she caught my cousin winking at me and her face hardened. 'He was always the gentleman,' she said, 'unlike some that I can see from here.'

Alec had a retort ready but I decided to jump in first. Not that I have any objection to people quarrelling in company, but I preferred the lady not to think that I was siding with my cousin against her. 'Did he keep house for himself?' I asked.

Again there was that tiny quiver of amusement. 'He had a housekeeper,' Alec said. 'The delightful Alice Nicholson. Came to him ten years ago, straight out of Do School . . .'

'Out of what?' I asked. I was beginning to follow more easily, but this was beyond me.

'College of Domestic Science,' Enterkin said.

'. . . and stayed with him ever since. Very loyal. Touching.'

'When you say yon last word,' Jim Fergus told him, 'smile.'

It was Mrs Grant who smiled, uncertainly. 'You're trying your best to fash me,' she said. 'But there was nothing between them.'

My cousin cocked an eye at her and her mouth tightened.

Somebody had to turn the conversation, but I had already done that duty once. I waited for the explosion which seemed inevitable, but Neil McDonald spoke up in the nick of time. 'What were you getting at in your evidence?' he asked Calder.

'Exactly what I told the sheriff,' Calder said. As if his thoughts had been written on a cartoonist's balloon over his head, I saw him wondering whether to say more and then deciding that a mysterious silence would be more provoking than to air the subject. 'Guns don't burst all that often,' he said, 'but I've seen more than my fair share of them and I've never known one go off like a bomb before. Damn it, not so long ago there was a man whose barrels parted company with the rest of the gun and went chasing after the bird. Even he walked away from it. I'm not saying that anything's wrong,' he added, 'just that the enquiry didn't delve deep enough.'

Old Hector Duffus pushed his plate away. 'You're fiking yoursel' o'ermuch,' he said.

'That's right,' Alec said. 'If he'd tripped and got his muzzle plugged with mud . . .'

'Where would he find mud in this weather?' Calder asked.

'There's no burn in that gulley?'

33

Regretfully, Duffus shook his head. 'But I've known a man load a twenty-bore cartridge ahead of a twelve-bore,' he said. 'If they both went off . . .'

'Did he ever shoot twenty-bore?' Calder asked.

Duffus shrugged.

'And he always loaded from his belt,' Mrs Grant said in her sugared voice. 'A twenty-bore cartridge would have fallen through the loops.'

This was mostly Greek to me; and Enterkin seemed equally bemused. But the others seemed to understand.

'I take it,' Calder said, 'that it wasn't his first shot of the day?'

'Ninth or tenth,' Jim Fergus said. 'You could tell if you could get hold of his belt. He filled it when we set out. So?'

'So that cuts out cleaning materials left in the bore. Tell me, in what size lots did he buy his cartridges?'

'You should know,' Alec said.

'My dear boy,' Enterkin said mildly, 'what on earth could that have to do with anything?'

Calder ignored the question. 'As far as I know, I never sold him any cartridges, although he could have bought some off my partner or one of our wives. I only want to know whether he usually bought a year's supply in bulk, or split a bulk order with a friend, or called in for a couple of boxes when he ran short.'

'Half a dozen boxes at a time,' Mrs Grant said. 'He was using some blue ones a few weeks ago, so your partner must have sold him a fresh lot.'

'So he couldn't have had them very long,' Calder said. 'Where did he keep them?'

'Under lock and key in his garage.'

'Near the central-heating boiler?'

'No,' she said. 'Not heated at all.'

'Damp?'

'A bittie. But,' she said irritably, 'like Mr Enterkin here, I don't see what you're getting at.'

'I'll explain. Cartridges tend to get dry at this time of year. Kept near central heating they get even drier. And the drier they get, the brisker. If you'd said that he kept them in the airing cupboard, or in the pocket of a coat hanging over a radiator, or that he'd had them for years in a dry house, I might have been less puzzled. Or, again, I might not.'

We had finished our coffee. The bill arrived. Neil McDonald picked it up and read out a staggering total, rounded it up for the tip and divided it by seven. Apparently we were going Dutch. And I had nothing like enough money on me nor anywhere else. Not only do authors get paid long in arrears; they do most of their work speculatively. Two of my potential blockbusters were doing the rounds of publishers without seeming to generate much enthusiasm.

But I was not going to let the heathen Scots know that the shoe was pinching. After a moment's frantic thought I produced my only credit card. 'I'll do this,' I said. 'I'm a long way from my bank.' And I picked up the cash which the others had put down. The cash would tide me over nicely and I would have about six weeks to find the money and save my bank manager from apoplexy. The tip which I left may not have been quite what was subscribed for it, but from the look of the waiter my need was greater than his.

As we got up from the table, Calder looked across at Duffus. 'For my own satisfaction,' he said, 'I'd like to visit the place where it happened.'

'Aye. If you must. But no' the day,' Duffus said. 'My accountant'll be waiting on me by now. Would Monday suit?'

'Fine,' Calder said.

He stepped back to let Mrs Grant go ahead, but she stopped in front of him. With her height, she could look him squarely in the eye. 'You misliked the treatment the sheriff gave you,' she said, 'but that's no reason to be making trachle for the rest of us. You watch your step. Go one inch over the line and you'll find yourself in a different kind of court.'

She swept towards the door.

'Trachle . . .' Enterkin began.

'. . . means trouble,' I finished for him. My friend at the hotel with the unreliable braces had included it in his lesson.

'So does Mrs Grant,' Calder said. 'She seems remarkably anxious for the verdict to stand.'

# FOUR

Walking back to the car, I found that my legs seemed disinclined to follow my careful instructions. Calder, who must have had a head like an anvil, took the wheel again; but I noticed that he kept to minor roads where the police were less likely to be lurking with their breathalysers at the ready. He also paid for a tankful of petrol without a murmur, which confirmed my impression that the two were old friends who bickered out of habit and without any real acrimony. I dozed for some of the way and woke with a headache and a mouth like a billygoat's crotch.

The solicitor, who had lunched with greater enthusiasm, was even more somnolent and Calder had to nudge him awake as we neared Newton Lauder. 'Mr Parbitter will stop off with me,' he said. 'I'll run him home later.'

Enterkin yawned. 'Very well,' he said.

'You can manage as far as the town?'

'Certainly.'

Calder turned off towards Newton Lauder, but soon turned again into a side-road which skirted an expanse of conifers. Beyond it, we arrived at an attractive nineteenth-century house which, despite its screen of taller trees, had a clear view down the valley to the town.

Enterkin declined an invitation to visit, moved into the driver's seat and drove slowly away. Calder watched until he was reasonably sure that the solicitor could stay on the road and then, carrying the jangling bag of bits, led me inside.

'Molly!' he called.

'Hullo?' A girl's voice from what I took to be the kitchen.

'I've brought Simon Parbitter back with me. Could we have some tea?'

'In the study. Two minutes.'

He left the bag in the hall and led me into the study, a panelled room in which he took evident pride. It was furnished with period pieces or good reproductions, glowing with polish, and the walls were almost obscured by shelves of books, some of them old, heavy, leather-bound and valuable-looking. They seemed to have been chosen for their contents rather than for their appearance. He waved me to a deep and comfortable leather chair.

Any ideas which I might have had about the life-style which a country gunsmith could afford were obviously due for revision. I was to realise later that Calder was far from typical. For a start, he was one of the country's foremost dealers in antique guns as well as an accomplished investigator and expert witness. And, although he never mentioned the fact, he was an authority on gun history whose occasional writings on the subject went round the world and were accepted for gospel.

He opened a corner cupboard. 'Could you manage a reviver?' he asked.

'Thanks,' I said, 'but no thanks. I need more practice before I can hope to compete with you chaps who were weaned on malt whisky.'

He nodded. 'You're probably wise,' he said. 'A cup of tea, something sugary and some deep breathing and you'll be fit to start again tonight.'

'God forbid!' I said.

Mrs Calder brought in a light tea-trolley. I struggled up from the depths of the chair to be introduced. Her voice had been a young girl's voice, but I saw that she was around forty. She had smiling eyes. She only came up to my chin, and because of her lack of inches the little flesh on her bones made her look plump, but plump in the cuddlesome and erotic way which some women can manage while others with similar build look just plain fat. She shook hands as if she meant it and sat down, knees tidily together but facing me.

'I've read some of your books,' she said. 'You look older than the photograph on your dust-jackets.'

'I am older than my photographs,' I pointed out. 'One has to be.'

'I suppose that's true.' The courtesies satisfied, she turned to her husband. 'How did it go?'

'About as we expected,' he said grimly. 'That oaf Cameron was

37

called as expert witness, which was about the only laugh of the day. He wrote it off as the normal result of using nitro cartridges in an old black-powder gun. I was only called as a witness to fact, so, although I tried to spread a little doubt around, my words of wisdom were discounted as being defensive. The sheriff obviously thought that guns are nasty, dangerous things anyway. He brought it in as an accident. He agreed that the law didn't prevent us selling nitro cartridges to Mr Hatton – which I swore that I hadn't done anyway. Somehow, that seemed to get overlooked when he made an oblique reference to the obligations of responsible traders.'

'Oh, Keith! What are you going to do?'

'Take it on the chin, probably. Just don't let me see any Scottish papers for the next few days. I've got the bits of the gun here. We'll take a look at them, and if I see the least chance of upsetting the verdict . . .'

Mrs Calder paused in the act of pouring. 'You could end up making some more enemies,' she said.

He nodded. 'Being right is the unforgivable sin,' he agreed. 'But being wrong is a worse one. You're either a fool or a troublemaker. Whichever way you look, the customers don't like it.'

They fell into silence, holding each other's eyes. They had the rapport which only a few of the very closest couples develop. Then the hostess in her took over, she unlocked her eyes and turned back to the guest, passing me my cup and a plate of sugary cakes.

'My daughter and I enjoy your detective novels,' she said. 'Why do you write so few?'

I decided that I liked her enough to tell the truth. 'They're useful pot-boilers,' I said, 'but they're damned hard work for all that they earn. In any other sort of fiction, say a love story, characters can be as illogical as you like because the average person isn't logical.'

'Especially in love,' she said, smiling.

'True,' I said. 'A mystery is different. If you're going to play fair with the reader, a whodunnit has to be logical, with no loose ends and factually accurate as well. And that's a real sweat.'

Calder humphed and his wife laughed at him. 'Debbie and I

always show Keith bits about guns in novels,' she said, 'because he turns purple and grinds his teeth when the author makes mistakes. But we weren't all brought up in the gun trade. I always tell him that when the details aren't part of the mainstream plot they don't matter. Most readers wouldn't know the difference.'

'I told Mr Calder that,' I said. 'And he said that that was all the more reason not to mislead them.'

'I never turn purple,' Calder said, amiably enough, 'just a pleasing shade of lavender. And I never grind my teeth. If you ever want to check the details, 'phone me. And I think you could call us Keith and Molly.'

'Thanks,' I said. 'I'll take you up on both your kind offers. I'm Simon, by the way. But the snag isn't what you don't know, it's what you think you do know. If you see what I mean.'

He nodded. 'I know exactly what you mean. It's true in all lines. It's true of that damned gun. I think I know what I'm doing. If I don't, the sharn will hit the fan. Ho-hum. Let's traipse upstairs, the three of us, and take a wee look at the bits. Bring your tea.'

So we traipsed. Carrying the bag, Keith led us up a broad, deeply carpeted stair. We waited while he did something secretive in a landing cupboard – unsetting burglar alarms, I guessed, when the red eyes of two sensors winked on as we entered a huge room made from two large bedrooms. When I turned to close the door behind us it moved so heavily that it had to be lined with steel plate. The reason for this security was obvious. Rack after mahogany rack held guns, two hundred at the least, and every one of them, to my untutored eye, an antique and perfect. At the total value I dared not even guess.

Keith glanced around. 'You see my problem,' he said. 'The value of every one of these depends on the customer believing that I'm infallible. And most of them are held on borrowed money.'

An L-shaped workbench, backed by tool-racks, occupied the corner between a window and the remainder of what had once been the dividing wall. Moving some work in progress, Keith cleared a space and laid out the remains of Uncle George's gun, placing the pieces in their proper relationship to each other. Some pieces were missing altogether, but I could see the shape which the gun should have taken.

39

Beside the pieces he laid another, complete gun. 'Ralph Enterkin left this with me,' he said. 'It's the twin. You can collect it if and when you get a shotgun certificate. Now . . .' He used a long gadget which had a dial at one end and two little wheels at the other and measured the internal diameter of the barrels of the good gun and then as much as remained of the other, muttering numbers aloud as he jotted them down. He repeated his work on the outside of the barrels with what I recognised as a micrometer.

'So much for that,' he said. 'If you want to sell the good one, I'll make you an offer. It won't be very much because of the risk that it would fail proof. My personal opinion, for what it's worth, is that submitting it for nitro proof would be a good gamble. You might lose a pair of barrels, but I think you'd have a better chance of gaining a much more valuable gun.' While he spoke, he was stowing the undamaged gun carefully in a leather case.

One of the racks was given over to antique pistols and had a cupboard underneath. From this cupboard, Keith began removing gun-barrels. 'I call this my Black Museum,' he said. 'I've been collecting burst barrels for years. This is one of the worst I've seen. He handed me a single barrel which had been ripped open for half its length. 'Late-eighteenth-century gun, only made as a decorative wall-hanger. Barrel of sham-dam – that's to say imitation Damascus, the pattern etched onto the outside of a cheap steel tube. Quite a common practice at one time. It gave Damascus its bad name and led to our proof laws. This was never meant to be fired, but some damn fool came by it and thought that he'd try it out with the powder from a nitro cartridge. He only lost one fingernail.

'Now this . . .' he handed me a pair of barrels with a gaping wound at one side '. . . resulted from a flaw in one barrel caused by the inclusion of some slag during its manufacture.'

He took the two specimens from me, laid them neatly on his bench and delved in the cupboard again. Examples came in quick succession. A barrel bulged like a doughnut around the jagged gap . . . typical obstructional burst . . .'; a pair with a bulging hole a few inches from the heavier end . . . 'twenty-bore case loaded in front of a twelve . . .'; and . . . just plain overloaded cartridge . . .'; until '. . . here's the one I was looking for . . .' he produced a pair of brown, attractively patterned barrels with a curl of metal sprung from the breech end.

'Damascus barrels,' he said, 'BP proof only, used for years with fairly heavy nitro cartridges. Comparable to your uncle's folly. When at last one of them gave up the ghost, this is what happened.'

I looked from one pair of barrels to the other but it was hard to make a comparison. In terms of a motor accident, it was like comparing a dented wing with a write-off.

'So. Do you see what I see?' Keith asked.

Molly and I exchanged a look of bafflement.

Downstairs, a door slammed. 'Here's Deborah home,' Keith said. 'She'll see it.' He went out onto the landing and called.

'The maddening thing,' Molly said, 'is that she probably will see whatever it is. She's been following Keith around like a puppy ever since she could toddle, watching everything he does and drinking up his every word. It's got so that when Abe Moray wants to trade in a bodged-up gun he waits until he sees her leave the shop before he'll go in.'

Deborah turned out to be a girl in her middle teens, the image of her mother except that she was coltish rather than plump. She had the same cheerfully outgoing manner and firm handshake. The bits on the bench drew her attention immediately. 'What on earth was it before that happened to it?' she asked.

'A semi-hammerless,' Keith said.

'Bentley patent?'

'That's right.'

'No wonder what's left of the lock-plates looked odd. Whose name's on it? Burgess?'

'Roper. Now,' Keith said, 'all three of you. Compare these records of human idiocy. Apart from the fact that Mr Hatton's gun is much worse damaged than the others, what strikes you? I don't want details. Just half-close the eyes and give me your impressions.'

We stood in silence, blearing through half-closed eyes at some bits of metal.

'I think I've got it,' Deborah said. (Her mother sighed.) 'The impression I've got is . . . speed. No, that's not the word I want. Suddenness, that's it.'

'Well done,' Keith said.

As soon as she spoke, I could see it. I could almost visualise the bursts in slow motion. The other barrels gave the impression that

41

as soon as the burst occurred the pressure had been released and the damage was over, but Uncle George's gun had been forced apart too suddenly for the expanding gases to relent.

'Could it have been an overload?' Deborah asked. 'With a magnum primer? And over-dried powder? Or . . . you remember the man who wrecked a Winchester rifle, using a pistol powder?'

'I doubt if it was any of those. We'll see,' Keith said. He studied the débris minutely and then looked at his fingers. 'I think I'll send some of these bits for analysis. There should be some residue impacted into them. Is Ronnie still planning to go to Edinburgh tomorrow?'

Molly nodded. 'He can take them.'

'OK,' Deborah said. 'Now that that's settled, can I talk to Mr Parbitter about his books?'

'I suppose so,' Molly said. 'But be gentle with him. He's taken a lot of stick from your father already. I'd better go and get on with the meal.' She looked at me. 'You'll stay?'

My watch suddenly told me that the afternoon was gone, the shops would be closing and I had still bought nothing for an evening meal. I was still feeling no more than convalescent, but food might prove to be the cure. 'If you're sure . . .' I began.

'I don't suppose these two will let you escape much before midnight,' she said. 'And my husband's partner and his wife are coming, so one more will be neither here nor there.'

'Then I'd like to stay,' I said.

She smiled and left the room.

'Take your jacket off,' Deborah said to me.

I probably said 'Huh?' or something very like it.

'Better do as she tells you,' Keith said, grinning. I took my jacket off and hung it on the back of the only chair.

'In *Scare*,' Deborah said severely, 'you had the hero leaping about in a well-cut suit and then suddenly producing a Colt forty-five. The revolver,' she added. I gathered that that made the heresy worse. 'Dad . . .?'

'We don't have a Colt in stock,' Keith said.

'Well, do you still have that Belgian copy of the Smith and Wesson Russian model? It's almost exactly the same size and weight,' she explained kindly. She bobbed down at the other end of the cupboard. One minute later, she had strapped me into a

42

holster containing what felt like a small field-gun. 'Now, while you try to get your jacket on over that, how many rounds of ammunition would he have been carrying?'

I thought back. I had forgotten the details of the book, but the shooting had occupied more than a chapter. 'Er . . . fifty?' I suggested.

She nodded and went down on her knees beside the cupboard. 'I'll let you off with fifty,' she said. 'Here we are. Two boxes of twenty-five. These are a bit lighter than the Colt, but they'll do. See if you can distribute them about your person.'

'I wouldn't,' Keith said, 'or that suit will never be the same again. The pockets will be dragging on the ground.'

'You've made your point,' I told Deborah gently.

'But I haven't yet,' she protested. 'The point I wanted to make is that everything else in your books comes over as so real that I can almost believe I'm really there. But when it comes to guns, your characters are only saying "Bang, bang, you're dead!" Do you see what I mean?'

'I hope so.'

'I don't think you do.' She looked at me with large, bright eyes while she thought about it. 'When the guns come out,' she said at last, 'they're cardboard cutouts. No weight, no bulk, no kick, no noise, no smoke.' She went down on her knees again before the cupboard and produced a smaller revolver and an automatic pistol. 'Dad, could we take a few of these out into the garden and do some shooting?'

Keith looked at the clock over the workbench. 'Not tonight,' he said.

'Oh, Dad!'

'I heard the doorbell go, so Janet and Wal are probably here. Mr Parbitter will come again.'

'You're sure?'

'He will if you don't nag him until he's got a scunner of the place.'

'I'll come,' I said. My mind was already filing away data for future books. 'So if I want a character to carry a hidden weapon, it should be an automatic pistol?'

Deborah nodded energetically. 'A small, flat one. Even then, it makes a bulge unless you wear it under something loose, like a shooting coat, the way Dad sometimes does.'

I could follow that side-issue up at some other time. 'How about in the pocket?' I asked. 'A bulge under the armpit would be a danger-signal, but a bulge in the pocket could be something quite innocent.'

'Don't try it with one up the spout unless you're very sure of a stiff safety-catch,' Keith said. 'Otherwise, when you want it out, you're pulling against the drag of the cloth and you can easily let it off. After which, it's almost certainly jammed and unusable.'

That suggested another detail for verisimilitude. 'And burn a hole in your jacket,' I said.

'Two holes,' Keith said. 'Both smouldering at the edges. A small one at the muzzle and another about two inches by an inch and a half opposite the ejector port. I did it myself once. I was lucky not to blow my balls off.'

'Or somebody else's.'

Keith shrugged. Clearly, that would have worried him less.

Keith's partner, Wallace James, was a lean man with lank hair and an occasional nervous stammer. I noticed that he was short of three fingers from his right hand. His manner was friendly but his wife, who was younger, blonde, a looker and not unaware of it, seemed reserved. This made me uneasy and I found myself tongue-tied, which at least had the benefit of preventing me from putting my foot in it while picking my way through the unfamiliar patterns of conversation.

Over drinks before the meal – Keith slipped me a port-and-brandy which I found wonderfully restorative to a thoroughly upset stomach – the Jameses, and Deborah when she joined us in a clean frock, wanted a word-by-word account of the enquiry and Keith obliged them. He had a gift as a raconteur and he made a funny story of it, but we could see that he was unhappy.

When the tale was told, Wallace James looked equally perturbed. 'You'll never learn,' he said.

'What would you have done?' Keith countered.

'Unless I was s-sure I could convince the court, I'd have stuck to answering the questions as asked.'

'I was sure,' Keith said. 'I just couldn't believe that the sheriff would accept the moronic drivelling that the idiot Cameron had been pouring into his ear.'

'Why wouldn't he, if the PF introduced Cameron as the expert witness?' Wallace sighed. 'And now you'll c-come over in the p-papers as irresponsible. And wrong.'

'For the moment,' Keith said. 'But, if there's any justice in the world, you're the one they'll pillory. Did you sell Simon's uncle nitro cartridges?'

'I haven't the faintest idea,' Wallace said. 'Ronnie picked up about a dozen boxes a few weeks ago. I thought that they were for Sir Peter, but he was as thick as thieves with Mr Hatton. Janet . . . ?'

'I don't know,' Janet said. 'What did your uncle look like?' she asked me.

'I hadn't seen him since I was a child,' I said. 'From memory, he was ten feet tall and about ten thousand years old.'

'There you are, Keith,' Wallace said. 'And you never told us not to, and if you had . . .'

'Yes?' Keith said. 'Would you have offended a customer?'

'Again, I'm damned if I know.'

The meal included a pie of a delicious meat which Molly said was woodpigeon, marinated in wine and simmered in a stock of her own devising. When we had finished, Molly, refusing all other assistance, carried Deborah off to help with the washing-up. We sat on at the dinner-table, too replete to bother moving.

Janet had been looking hard at Keith. 'I think he's preparing to get up to something,' she told her husband. 'Keith, what are you planning to do?'

'I'd like to look into it a little further,' Keith said, very softly.

Wallace sat up and glared at him. 'You'd do more harm than good. And we're too busy.'

'All I'm proposing,' Keith said, 'is to send some parts of the gun for spectrographic analysis of the residue. If the analyst says "Nitro powder", that's an end to the matter. And I've already arranged with Hector Duffus that we can go and look at the place on Monday. That's not unreasonable, since we stand accused of selling the lethal cartridge.' He was speaking very gently, but suddenly I knew that he was going to do exactly what he wanted to do, whatever the reactions of the others.

'From your standpoint, it may be quite reasonable,' Janet said. 'But you look at the world through your own rather peculiar eyes and you don't see the same things other folk do. Whatever you do, others will see it as prying and mischief-making.'

'What's more,' Wallace said, 'we know you. You'll c-convince yourself you're on to s-something and go haring off, just when we're coming to the busiest time of the year.'

Keith smiled and looked up at the ceiling. 'Nobody would raise an eyebrow,' he said dreamily, 'if Simon were to look into his uncle's death.'

He was wrong. Wallace raised an eyebrow. But he lowered it again. 'No,' he said. 'I don't suppose they would.'

My eyebrows, on the other hand, seemed to have got stuck somewhere close to my hairline. I wondered whether this was not the reason for all the help and hospitality. 'I've no experience as an investigator,' I said.

'You write detective stories,' Janet pointed out.

'That's different. You start from the other end.'

'But they're logical and deductive,' Wallace said.

'And Keith and his family have spent the whole day convincing me that I know nothing about guns.'

'It'll be a grand way to learn something,' Keith said. 'Think it over. We can't do anything useful for a day or two.'

'You might even get a book out of it,' said Deborah.

That, I admitted to myself, was a good point. But there was a snag. 'I'll have to start writing something very soon,' I said. 'I've got a tax instalment to pay in January and if I don't get a publisher's advance by then I shan't be able to pay it. They'll probably jug me.'

'You could get another book out of that,' Janet said. Hers was always the tongue with the barb.

Until then, Wallace had been looking at me vaguely, as if unsure whether I were really there, but now he focused on me. He asked half a dozen penetrating questions about my financial state, questions which I would have resented from anyone who was not taking such an intense but obviously impersonal interest in my answers. Wallace, I was to learn, had been an accountant until the loss of his fingers made the profession impracticable and he was passionately interested in money, not for its own sake but as counters in sporting challenges with other businessmen, and, most particularly, with the tax officials.

When he had a broad picture of my finances, he was scowling.

'What bungling idiot do you employ for an accountant?' he asked.

'I do my own tax returns,' I said.

He was strong-minded enough to refrain from scoring the point. 'And you just tell them how much you earned and let them help themselves?'

'I claim for my materials,' I said with dignity, 'and for travelling to the library. I even get an allowance for the part of my flat I write in.'

'They've had you for a sucker,' Wallace said. I noticed that his stammer had disappeared. 'Just for a start, where did you last go on holiday?'

'Tenerife,' I said. That trip had been the product of a burst of extravagance triggered by the unusual arrival of two separate cheques, when I had far greater need to trade in my word processor for an up-to-date model.

'And did you write about it?'

'No.'

'Did you even think about using it as a background?'

'Well,' I said, 'yes.'

'Then it's deductible.'

'We'd never get away with it. My girlfriend was with me,' I explained.

'She wasn't your girlfriend, she was your secretary,' Wallace announced. 'Bring me your tax papers for the last few years as soon as you can get them and I promise you that you won't have to worry about next January, nor the one after.'

I thought that I was probably being blackmailed. 'And if I decide that I'm not cut out to be Keith's investigative assistant?'

'That's nothing to do with it. I'll be happy with ten per cent of what I can claw back for you. Deal?'

'Deal,' I said. In a momentary glow of optimism I accepted another glass of wine and followed it with a brandy.

It was arranged that the Jameses would run me home. Before we left, Keith handed me a small but heavy parcel to deliver to his brother-in-law. We stopped at a neat little house, within the boundaries of the town and yet set apart by the trees which flourished on an unbuildable slope of rock, but there was nobody there. I took the parcel home with me. I was already thinking of Tansy House as home.

47

# FIVE

As I drifted off to sleep that night, I found myself thinking about the ego, that sense of personal identity by which each of us knows himself from all others. There had been a group of us at dinner. Each of us had, to himself or herself, been 'Me'. Why was I the one trapped in this particular body, with these problems and these blessings now; these uncertainties about the future; and these frailties and this death, whatever and whenever they might be, still to come? Surely there were the makings of a story there. But as it began to take form I fell asleep, and in the morning most of it was gone.

A knock at the door came while I was at my breakfast in the morning. In truth, I was glad of the excuse to give up trying to coax a few flakes of milky cereal down my reluctant throat. Calder sociability was hard on the liver and gut.

There was a Land-Rover parked in the road. It was battered, mud-stained and rusty. The large and untidily dressed man who had knocked seemed to be in much the same state. Not that he was actually rusting, but he looked as if he very well could be – his big frame had the kind of solidity that suggests cast iron and his face could have been carelessly welded from scrap metal.

'I'm Ronnie,' he said. The name conveyed nothing to me. 'Ronnie Fiddler,' he added. And, when I still failed to catch on, 'Keith's brother-in-law.' The use of that terminology, rather than referring to himself as Molly's brother, said a lot for Keith's dominance of his immediate circle.

There was something which I was supposed to remember, but it was all too much effort at that stage of the morning. 'You'd better come in and have a coffee,' I said.

'I'll do that,' he said. But when he had joined me in the kitchen he changed his mind. 'I'll sooner tak' a beer if you've got it,' he said. 'I've an a'fu drouth.'

I guessed that he meant an awful thirst. I felt much the same. The idea of beer for breakfast was slightly shocking, but I fetched a can from the refrigerator and when I had poured it into a glass – a refinement which he seemed to feel unnecessarily fastidious – it looked so fresh that I got out another for myself. To my surprise it went down more easily than the cereal and did more good.

Ronnie took a pull at his beer and burped appreciatively. 'You've a grand wee place here,' he said.

'Aye,' I replied. Local idiom rubs off on me very quickly.

'Yon shaw at the back, that's a good roosting wood.'

'Glad to hear it,' I said, wondering what on earth he was talking about.

'You'll not be, when you see what the cushats do to your garden.' He paused and scratched his ear. 'Thing is, your uncle aye let me have a crack at the cushie-doos. I'm wondering would you do the same?'

I hated to admit that he had me baffled but we had passed the stage at which nodding and smiling would suffice. He began again, carefully. 'The cushats – woodpigeon – roost in your wood back there. I'd like fine to have your permission to shoot them of an evening. I'll give you a few for the pot,' he added.

'I'm sorry,' I said, 'but no. I don't approve.'

'Whit for no'?' he asked reasonably. 'It's no' cruel, if that's what you're thinking. It's a kinder death than they'll find in nature.'

'Maybe,' I said. 'But have you ever considered what it does to you? Don't you become harder, more brutal?'

I had expected this rough character to discount the idea with the contempt which it probably deserved. He surprised me by making a movement which was somewhere between a nod and a shake of the head. 'I'd wondered that myself,' he said. 'See, I'm a stalker to trade. But I think not. You grow up thinking what your mum tells you to think. "Leave that, it's dirty . . . dinna' dae that, it's cruel." All that happens is you grow out of a' that and learn to act natural, else you go through life dafter than nature intended. I've more often thought that the man who can't bear to kill and clean his own meat's no right to eat meat at a'. Now then!'

'You're advocating the perpetuation of brutality,' I said.

'Maybe I am and maybe I'm no'. But it's not from among us that the vandals and the football hooligans come.'

I could see that he had a point although I was damned if I was going to concede it. 'I'm not convinced,' I said.

He shrugged. 'It's a matter for yourself,' he said. 'But you'll have Sir Peter at you.'

I was less interested in who might be 'at me' than in his reference to my uncle. Wallace had suggested that the two had been as thick as thieves. 'You knew my uncle well?' I asked.

'Well enough.'

'Did you buy some boxes of cartridges for him recently?'

Ronnie grinned and then looked solemn. 'I did that. He said that it was because I get a discount, but I thought that it was because Keith had read him the riot act about using nitro cartridges in his old guns. A lot of daft nonsense I thought it at the time, but it seems Keith may've had the right of it.'

'Was my uncle through here often?' I asked.

'Whenever he felt like a break from the farm. On an arable farm,' he explained, 'you're busy for much of the year but, whiles, there's little to do but wait for land to dry or crops to grow. He liked the company better around here. He'd leave your cousin to keep an eye on the twa-three men that he had, come through and, in the season, he'd shoot wi' Sir Peter. Out of it, he'd come out wi' me and the ferrets. Some nights we'd make up a party for a roost-shoot, taking along any guest he'd got here. And there were times I could fix him up with a bit of stalking.'

'He brought guests here, did he? Who do you remember?'

'I didn't pay them much heed. 'Course, there was his fancy woman. The farmer's widow. He was seldom here but she was along.'

'Mrs Grant?'

'That's the one. A damned fine woman, seemed to me. A good shot in the daytime and a grand target by night, I'm thinking. Then there was a mannie as was a builder. McDonald, that was his name.'

'And two farmers?' I asked. Hector Duffus, in his evidence, had stated that the five had often shot together.

'More'n two,' Ronnie said. 'Seemed more like there was dozens

50

of the buggers. Well, being a farmer hisself, his friends would mostly be the same.' He finished his beer. 'Now, if you've got Keith's wee parcel I'd better be getting along.'

It came back to me that he was here to collect the bits of gun. In my debilitated state, the memory had refused to surface. I fetched the small parcel. He thanked me for the beer, promised to buy me one in return if I was ever in the Canal Bar, and made a noisy departure.

My breakfast had gone mushy but the beer had restored my appetite. I finished my cereal and washed up. Uncle George's washing-up gloves were old and stained yellow so I threw them out. I was considering work – as a general concept rather than as anything specific – when the phone rang.

'The funeral will be tomorrow,' said Mr Enterkin's voice without preamble. 'Friday. Two p.m.'

'I'll be there,' I said.

'Well, I won't. I would usually attend a client's funeral, but I have a meeting which can hardly be postponed. I would be grateful if you'd make that clear, should anybody remark on my absence.'

'I'll do that,' I said. 'Where is it?'

He gave me directions and then returned to the matters on his mind. 'It is the custom,' he said, 'for the close relatives to take the principal mourners for a meal after the funeral. I have discussed the matter with your cousin. I gather that neither of you is too well endowed at present, so, since his legacy is by far the larger, I have made him a modest advance against it. He will see to the matter.'

My relief at not being stuck with another large lunch-bill was tempered by embarrassment that my financial state should be generally known.

'There is one other thing,' Enterkin said. 'If you are dependent on your motorcycle for transport you may well not feel like a long ride back here after an occasion which may well prove somewhat . . . exhausting. A bed will be available at Kirkton Mains Farm, if you should so wish.'

'Very thoughtful of somebody,' I said.

'Your cousin. You have not, I suppose, come to any conclusion about whether you intend to retain Tansy House? I would like to know how to proceed.'

'I haven't had time to think about it,' I said, although I had done more than a little thinking on the subject without being sure which option I fancied less – returning to the impersonal congestion of London, but with a healthy balance to cushion my future, as against settling rent-free in a landscape not entirely flattened and perfumed by other people's feet to build a new life among strangers with strange customs and an unfamiliar mode of speech. 'I'll let you know,' I said, and concluded the conversation.

According to the radio, London was still roasting in the unusual heat, but when I put my head outside I found that the sunshine was tempered by a cooling breeze. The light was clear and sharp compared to London's faint haze and I felt that I could have picked out every blade of grass on the further hills.

I was in that hesitant state which comes over a man when he has so many things to do that it is impossible to decide which to do first. To clear my mind pending a sensible decision, I got out the bike and ran into Newton Lauder for some shopping. On the narrow road most traffic tended to hold the middle unless confronted by an oncomer. There was a nasty blind hump not far from Tansy House where a tractor and trailer gave me a fright, but the rest of the road was straight and a flat-out run in both directions helped to blow away the cobwebs and my frustrations with them. I returned with food and a fresh pair of washing-up gloves. Any distraction, such as from chapped hands, can spoil my concentration.

Back at the house I put some paper beside my uncle's old typewriter. Sometimes the sight of an invitingly blank sheet will conjure up words to fill it, but not this time. I got up and prowled around.

The house was still imprinted with my uncle's life and personality. Personal odds and ends, from pipes and tobacco to reading glasses, lay where he had left them. Whether I stayed or went, it would have to be sifted through. I found some cardboard cartons, probably dating from a delivery of groceries, and made a start.

As is so often the case with other people's possessions, there was a substratum of oddments which might have been retained for souvenir value or because they had some now forgotten purpose or just in case they might some day come in useful for mending something. Anything of obvious use or value I left in its place. The rest I divided between papers which should be stored away; junk which could safely be discarded; and a middle category of things which I did not want but which might, for somebody else, have a use or value.

I started in what had been my uncle's bedroom and was now, for the moment, mine. Saving such of his clothing as fitted me and might be worn without too comical an effect, I boxed the rest to be given to some jumble sale. Behind the suits and jackets on their hangers I found a smart black cocktail dress. Putting aside any thought that my uncle might have been transvestite, I decided that this had belonged to Emily Grant. A lady who was a frequent visitor and liked to be prepared – Mrs Grant did not look as if she had ever been a Brownie but you never knew – might well have left provision against a sudden social need.

The fact that this had turned up in my uncle's bedroom did not smirch the lady's reputation. It would, after all, have been less in the way there than in the wardrobe of the spare bedroom, whence it would have to be removed to suit the next visitor. But, as I worked on, I realised that I had been able to stow away my own luggage so easily because Uncle George had meticulously kept vacant an exact half of the drawers in his chest and in the dressing-table, half the wardrobe and one of the bedside cabinets. Half of the mirrored cabinet in the bathroom was similarly reserved. I decided that, as far as I was concerned, Mrs Grant could consider her reputation well and truly smirched after all. The bed in which I was passing my nights had known some elderly extra-marital shenanigans.

The spare bedroom had been kept empty, only needing sheets and a towel to be ready for immediate use by other visitors. A wash-basin had been installed in a corner and the soap in its dish was dry but not hard.

Downstairs, after a sketchy lunch, I made a start on the living–dining room. This ran the depth of the house and had windows on to both the road and the garden. The pattern of the good carpet and the delicately fussy armchairs would have been legacies from my aunt, but other traces of her presence had vanished and the room was now comfortably masculine.

I was interrupted by another visitor in another of those ubiquitous Land-Rovers, made necessary, I was realising, by a spacious countryside in which not everywhere could be served by Tarmac. This time, the Land-Rover was brightly painted in several colours, unblemished and lovingly polished, but the visitor was little smarter than his predecessor. He was, in fact the scarecrow whom I had seen in Ralph Enterkin's outer office, for whose benefit the solicitor had hurried to get rid of me. He was still wearing the kilt.

'Mr Parbitter?' he said. 'My name's Hay.'

I might not have recognised the name if his vowels, even in so few words, had not betrayed the accent of class and education. 'Sir Peter Hay?' I said.

'Er, yes. That's right.'

I invited him in. As he stepped up into the hall I realised that he was taller than I, although just as thin. His grey hair was long, naturally curly and not very recently brushed. His face and hands – and, I noticed as he sat down, his knees – were reddened, as if he had been making the most of the sunshine.

'I was sorry about your uncle's death,' he said formally. He had the slightly whinnying voice which sometimes goes with that accent.

'So was I,' I said, 'although I hadn't seen him for years. Did you know him well?'

He considered the question, and then shrugged. 'I liked him rather better than I knew him,' he said. 'We got on well. I hadn't seen him for about a month before his death although he was in residence here at the time he died. I'd been away and he didn't manage to get through here as often as he liked.'

'I heard that he shot with you,' I said.

'That's true. We sometimes got together for a little rough shooting and occasionally he turned out for a day with the syndicate.' He gave me a probing glance under eyebrows as shaggy as his hair. 'I meant to work round gently to this, but since the subject's in the open . . . I have most of the shooting around here, but your uncle's few acres, now yours, would have made an awkward hole in it, let alone the wood being ideal for releasing a

54

few pheasants. In return for the use of it, he was welcome to come along as an extra gun any time that he could get here on a shooting day and he had standing permission to go after the bunnies or pigeons on my land. He was always meticulous about letting me know, which is how we sometimes came to go out together. Unfortunately, we only had a gentleman's agreement about your uncle's patch. I'm hoping that you'll honour it.'

'But I don't shoot,' I said.

'Ah. Then an annual rent in lieu?'

'I didn't realise that I was in the middle of a shoot,' I said. 'I'm a writer. Does this mean that I'll have shooting all around me?'

'About once every two weeks at the most, late October to January. The guns would be beyond the wood, and only for an hour or so each fortnight. What do you say?'

'It's against my principles,' I said. 'I'm sorry.' And I was, although more for the lost revenue than for him. It was not that I really identified myself with his pheasants, I was just generally hostile. Until that moment I had felt like a stranger in a strange land, and finding that I had some rights had gone to my head. That, and a dislike of having a landowner stereotype looking at me as if he expected me to tug my forelock. My experience of London landlords had not been happy.

'We've already put out two hundred poults on your uncle's say-so,' he said sadly. 'If you won't even honour the agreement until January . . . would you sell me the whole place? On valuation?'

'If I decide to sell, I'll let you know.'

'I'd be grateful. Well, I suppose you're entitled to your opinions,' he said, getting up and moving towards the door. 'I'll have the release pen removed and we'll start shifting the feeders and water-points a few yards each day and see if we can coax the birds over the boundary.' He halted on the threshold. 'You do realise that there would be very little conservation of wildlife if it weren't for the shooting man?'

'I'll take your word for it,' I said.

'And it doesn't influence you?'

His courtesy, and the fact that he seemed to have right on his side, had only aggravated my stubbornness. 'To be brutally frank,' I said, 'I don't know what all the fuss is about wildlife. Is

55

our life any the poorer because the dodo died out? I'll tell you this,' I went on, with a maliciously inspired flight of imagination, 'man is the only creature that deliberately preserves his competitors.'

I shut the door rudely on his astonished face, because my mind was taken up with wondering whether I could get a starting-point for a plot out of the thought, and deciding reluctantly that I couldn't. And my guts were troubling me again. Well, I could make my peace with him some other time. I headed for the bathroom.

# SIX

The women in my life had had their accomplishments but not one of them had been able to do more in the kitchen than open a tin. I had had to learn to cater for myself in a lazy, bachelor sort of way. I fried steak and followed it with some fruit before tackling the study.

Keith Calder arrived before I was half-finished. I let him in, led the way into the living room and pointed to an armchair before I realised that he had not followed. I found him poking around in one of the cartons in the hall.

'Are these for keeping or for throwing out?' he asked.

I said that that was my 'somebody might want it but I don't' box.

He recovered some oddly shaped tubes and gadgets from it. 'These are hand-loading tools for twelve-bore cartridges,' he said. 'Which seems a bit odd when you remember that your uncle didn't heed my warnings and seems to have been buying factory-loads.' He examined them carefully. 'They don't seem to have been used much if at all. I'd hang on to them if I were you – at least until we've finished our investigation. Then I'll sell them for you.'

I let the assumption of a joint endeavour go past and returned the tools to the table in the corner of the study which seemed to have served as a makeshift workbench, good enough for minor jobs in a second home. He followed me into the study and took a good look around, sniffing at a yellow stain on the worktable and picking a match out of the ashtray – really, his curiosity was almost intolerable – and when at last I managed to lead him into the living room he shied away from the chairs and went to stand at the window overlooking the garden. The low evening light

57

showed the border of shrubs in flower and the vegetables beyond the patch of lawn to good advantage. Unfortunately it also showed up the haze of small weeds which was appearing between the plants, the over-long grass and the raggedness of the vegetables where the pigeon had been feasting.

His nosiness irritated me, but I did owe him hospitality. I offered him a drink and he enquired tactfully whether I'd got around to laying in some whisky. As it happened, Uncle George had left behind a selection of bottles which would stand me in good stead in an area where conversation seemed to be impossible without the lubrication of refreshment. I poured a 'drappie' for each of us and, by placing his drink beside one of the chairs, forced him to sit down at last.

Beside my own chair I had put a few papers for further study. On an impulse I handed him what, from the legend, was a plan of Kirkton Mains Farm. 'What do you make of the scribbles?' I asked him.

He pored over it for a few seconds and then laughed. 'OSR would be oilseed rape,' he said, 'and I suppose KP would be Kerr's pinks, a potato variety. Your uncle was sketching out his planting plan.'

'He's drawn a line round a fat triangle in the top right-hand corner.'

He studied the plan for a minute before commenting. 'It encloses a couple of small woods and an old quarry,' he said at last. 'My guess is that that area's reserved for his pheasants. The two bits of field inside that line would be for planting with crops to help hold them. Jerusalem artichokes, maybe – it doesn't say. He seems to have retained his hedgerows and some other tree-strips around the farm, so his thrift as a farmer didn't extend to ruining the shooting. Does your cousin shoot?'

'I don't think so,' I said.

'You might find out, at the funeral tomorrow.'

'So might you,' I pointed out.

He shook his head. 'I was in two minds about going but I don't want to give anybody too much food for thought. Or reason to believe that I feel any guilt.'

That reminded me. 'I haven't seen a paper today,' I said. 'Did you get a bad press?'

'About what I expected. Some honest reporting of the sheriff's remarks, one or two snide comments and a stirring of the anti-gun fanatics.' He sighed. 'I dare say I'll live it down, but I'll live it down a damned sight quicker if we can show that something was tampered with.'

'Is that why you were interested in those tools?' I asked.

He looked at me as if I were an idiot, which on that subject and compared to himself I suppose I was. 'Well, of course,' he said. 'What else? If somebody tampered with a cartridge, they had to use tools. The modern cartridge isn't closed with a card and a turnover like the old ones, it's closed with a crimp, which is just a way of folding. You can open it easily enough with something like an ordinary wood-screw, but closing it again, and so neatly that the user wouldn't notice anything amiss, would require either very clever fingers or the proper tools.'

'But surely,' I said, 'if something like that happened – which I don't for a moment accept – why would it have happened here?'

'No reason,' he said. 'Except that a doctored cartridge would have had to have been put into his belt, and this seems to be one of the three most likely places. It was just thinking about it and then seeing the tools ... You could ask whether he ever used them and where they came from.'

'I suppose I could.'

'There's not much else to be done until the report comes back from the analyst. Deborah wants to know when you're coming back to do some handgun shooting.'

The proposal was attractive and yet daunting. 'Must I?' I asked. 'Guns make me nervous.'

'They make most people nervous until they know something about them,' he said. 'After that, they realise that it's people you have to be nervous about, not guns. Yes, I think you should. Deb was saying this morning that, like most writers, you make the bullet hit or miss according to what you want for the plot, irrespective of range, calibre or the skill of the marksman. A little practical experience would stand you in good stead for ever after.'

'I suppose that's perfectly true,' I said.

He nodded. 'Ralph Enterkin says you're probably staying over at the farm tomorrow night. Come and see us on Saturday afternoon. Stay for dinner.'

'I'd like that,' I said truthfully.

He sat for an hour and downed two more whiskies but I could

not grudge them to him. He was an amusing talker. In between priming me with questions to be asked of my uncle's friends if the chance should arise, he talked about guns, producing a fund of historical anecdotes. I found my writer's instinct stirring.

'One other thing,' he said suddenly. 'More than one cartridge may have been tampered with. Say an intruder found your uncle's belt empty, he'd have to leave it the same. And one cartridge in one box might not get used for months. So he might have doctored one in each box. I'd better take them away and examine them.'

Just before he left, we got on to the subject of gunpowder. Early and dangerous problems, he said, had been solved when the powder was mixed wet, dried and then 'corned' but much superstitious dispute had arisen over the liquid to be used. 'Some said that urine was best,' he said. 'Fussier souls preferred the urine of a bishop, while the perfectionists insisted on the urine of a wine-drinking bishop.' He looked at his watch and got to his feet. 'Is that the time? I must go or Molly will fret.'

I fetched my uncle's stock of cartridges. 'You can't have had many wine-drinking bishops in Scotland,' I said.

'You'd be surprised.' As he shrugged on his coat, he hesitated and then said, 'If you're short of money, you have some sellable things here.'

The comment was kindly meant so I decided not to take offence. 'I've looked around,' I said. 'I didn't see anything which would fetch more than junk prices.'

He pushed a coat aside and showed me the walking-sticks below. Not yet needing a stick, I had paid them no attention. Now I saw that the handles were beautifully carved. One which I noticed showed the head of a goose while another, more elaborate, had a labrador's head holding a dead pheasant in its mouth. 'Your uncle used to carve these. He liked to sit at his fireside of an evening with the television going, and work away quietly on one of them. He used to come to me for scrap offcuts of walnut and I know that he visited a lot of craftsmen in search of exotic timbers and other materials. I told him I could sell them for fifty quid a time, but he wasn't interested. He liked to give them away, but only to people he really liked, or so he said. He may have been flanelling me. I have one and I'm proud of it.'

There were five sticks in the rack. 'I'm glad you told me,' I said. 'I might easily have given them away. They could furnish me with a cushion until Mr James gets me a rebate.'

'That's not all.' He pulled out a stick which differed from the others, clicked something near the handle and pulled. The stick extended and a long slot appeared. 'Walking-stick gun.'

'I'll be damned,' I said. 'Who'd want one of those?'

'They're not uncommon. Poachers and gamekeepers mostly. But sometimes the laird liked his walking-stick to be shootable, for self-defence. This is a cut above most of them, ivory handle and gold furniture. Treat it with care and speak to me before parting with it.'

I studied the strange weapon with interest. 'It has a rubber ferrule for putting to the ground,' I said.

'It pulls off, but if you were in a hurry you could shoot it off without doing any damage.'

'Ought I to have this?' I asked.

'Strictly, no. If you left it with me I couldn't give it back to you without seeing your shotgun certificate. As it is . . . I haven't seen it.' He looked into the open breech and then dug into his coat pocket, produced several cartridges, isolated two which were smaller than the others and tried one for size. 'As I thought,' he said. 'Four-ten.' He dropped the cartridges into the dish of oddments which stood on the hall table, winked at me and turned to the door. 'It might be fun to do some ballistic tests,' he said thoughtfully.

'On the walking-stick gun?'

'I was thinking more of a wine-drinking bishop against a whisky-drinking minister. We could settle the question once and for all.' His big grin vanished into the new darkness.

A lorry rumbled past. I was hardly aware of it. I was standing in the hall, opening and closing the walking-stick gun. It was a fascinating piece, beautifully made and both light and comfortable to the hand. A safety-catch was hidden among some fancy scroll-work and when this was moved a slim trigger emerged from the handle.

But why had Keith left the cartridges? Was it a subtle way of inclining me towards shooting? Did he think that I might need to protect myself? Or was he acting on the principle that if you have a gun you should be able to shoot it? I would have to ask him, although his answer would be evasive.

The lorry rumbled back towards Newton Lauder, making the ornaments jingle.

The stick with the goose's head handle fitted my hand at just the right height. I decided to keep it for my own, selling the others. Living in the country, I would need a stick. If I decided to stay . . .

I was back at my uncle's desk, wondering what Keith had found significant about the spent matches, when the knocking began at the front door, laboured and yet insistent. There was something strange about it and I felt the hair rise on my neck. As I went to the door it came again and the sound came from low down. As if somebody were crouching. Or some animal, unable to reach the bell . . .

I loaded the walking-stick gun, pulled the rubber ferrule off the end and slipped the safety-catch. With my finger on the trigger, I tiptoed to the door and jerked it open suddenly, pointing the gun out into the darkness.

The outside light was still on and more light spilled from the door. There was nobody in front of me.

'Don't shoot,' said a hoarse voice, seemingly from between my feet. I jumped. If, in my fright, my bowels let loose a noise it was drowned by the sound of the shot as, involuntarily, I pulled the trigger.

Keith was lying at my feet, dirty, rumpled and showing traces of blood. I knelt down beside him.

'Don't move me,' he said quickly. 'I've a busted leg and I'm not too sure of one of my wrists. Run off the road by a lorry, at that blind hump in the road.'

I left him while I phoned for an ambulance and then went back with a cushion for his head. I reloaded the walking-stick gun and kept it handy. 'You crawled all that way?' I asked stupidly.

'It was that or wait to be found, maybe by somebody I wouldn't want to find me. It wasn't too bad, on my back and using my elbows and one leg.' Keith stopped and seemed to have fainted. I waited and his voice suddenly came back, stronger. 'He was waiting beyond the hump and came straight at me, only putting his lights on at the last minute. Deliberate as hell. I had to leave

62

the road or hit him head-on. The hatchback had an argument with a rock and lost out. It's a write-off. I'd just crawled as far as the roadside when I heard him coming back. I thought I was for it, but he drove past.' Keith's voice was getting fainter again. 'Could I have some water?'

I fetched water and helped him to drink.

'Phone my wife,' he said. 'Make it clear I'm in no danger. And ... can I leave you to deal with the fuzz?'

'Yes, of course,' I said.

'I couldn't get a number, there was mud on his plates. And there didn't seem to be a name on the lorry. It was about an eight-tonner, probably Leyland, neither light nor dark. And that's about all I can say. Tell 'em all I've told you, but you needn't put too much emphasis on its being deliberate. If they start making a connection with the other business, play it down. They probably won't, but if they do ... tell them that my favourite suspect's the local super ... chap called Munro. He's been calling down doom and damnation on me for years.'

'You don't really think ...?' I began.

'Not a chance. But it should cause a distraction. And, listen, 'phone Ledbetter's garage and tell them to collect the remains.'

There were a thousand questions that I wanted to ask, but he had talked enough and the ambulance, which only had a few miles to come, arrived a minute or two later. As the men opened the stretcher beside him he spoke once more. 'Come on Sunday as arranged,' he said. 'Or, if they're still keeping me, come and see me in dock. Now you'll just have to take over.'

The ambulance carried him away, leaving me to get on with all the chores which follow an accident.

# SEVEN

Another day dawned bright and warm.

One 'phone-call was enough to establish that Keith was no more badly damaged than he had supposed. A simple fracture had been set and encased, and a wrist taped. He would be home within the next day or two. In a conversation relayed by a nursing sister with a bog-Irish voice, he asked whether I could use a camera and whether I had one. I said, Yes but not with me, and the sister then said that Mr Calder would like me to visit his wife, so he would.

The visit, it turned out, was not to give aid or comfort but so that Molly could lend me an expensive camera, with instructions for its use and admonitions to treat it with the greatest care. Keith's injuries she was inclined to shrug off, although shadows under her eyes spoke of a sleepless night. Apparently such mishaps were common coin in the Calder household, but I decided that she was hiding a deep concern behind a façade of 'business as usual'.

I rode the Yamaha northward, following by memory the map and Mr Enterkin's directions, in an anxious mood. Of course, Keith's imagination might well, in the circumstances, have been running away with him. But if he were right, and his crash had been no accident but a deliberate attack on him, had it been to prevent him looking deeper into the shooting tragedy? And, if I asked questions, would I become next in the firing-line?

The two constables who had followed up the happenings of the night had seemed to feel that Keith was probably framing an excuse for his insurance company but that, if not, he had made more than enough enemies over the years to account for any number of murderous attacks. They refused Uncle George's

64

whisky but accepted hot sandwiches and mugs of tea while hinting at a series of escapades which had more than once endangered his life and his licence as a firearms dealer.

The breakdown vehicle had already been attached to the remains of the Calders' car when I went by. I had had to concede to myself that that was exactly where I would have placed an ambush, if so inclined. On the other hand, a pair of innocent headlights suddenly appearing over the crest could have produced the same results. Except that the lorry – a lorry, I corrected myself – had driven past the wrecked car, unseeing or uncaring, as he lay injured at the roadside.

The graveyard was high on a hill, divorced from the church in the nearby village. There was a large turnout; mostly, I guessed, of locals. My cousin shook hands very solemnly when I arrived. Mrs Grant and the three shooting men were grouped at the head of the grave.

An elderly minister took the short service. He sounded sincere and almost convincing as he spoke of Uncle George's prospect of eternal life, but I found my attention wandering to the distant view over the Forth estuary and out to sea. My cousin, the two farmers, Neil McDonald and I took the ropes. The sixth was taken by a small, stout man in rough serge. McDonald had to change places with me in order to spare his injured shoulder. As the coffin went down there was a sudden flight of birds overhead and I saw the shooting men look up, and felt them hesitate. Or perhaps, I thought, Uncle George had stirred.

The men retrieved their sticks. Alec, Jim Fergus and the stout man were using sticks which looked like my uncle's work, and there were others to be seen among the mourners. Duffus and McDonald had plainer, utilitarian sticks and Mrs Grant no stick at all. If they had been favoured recipients of Uncle George's handiwork, surely they would have shown respect by carrying them at his funeral?

After the service and the usual slow milling-around for a chat, the crowd moved to the larger and more up-market of the village pubs where we were to lunch. I left the 'bike where it was and walked down. Drinks were circulating. The majority took to the whisky but I had learned my lesson and stayed with sherry. Unidentified faces appeared, made conventional noises of commiseration and vanished again. A recurring remark was, 'When yon flock of cushats went over I was half-expecting old George to sit up and take a crack at them.' Cushats, or cushie-doos, I knew from Ronnie, were woodpigeon. I sensed, without any firm reason, that the affection for my uncle had been genuine and not a posthumous pretence.

The lunch-party moved through into a dining room. I found myself sharing a small table with Mrs Grant and the stout man. Mrs Grant looked just right in a grey dress and with no jewellery. She was polite and even friendly. Her annoyance at Keith was forgotten or had not rubbed off on me. Cousin Alec was bustling about, the epitome of the perfect host, and came to offer more drinks. The stout man was introduced as Wally Ritchie, my uncle's foreman and tractor-driver. He stayed with the pint of beer which he had brought through with him. Mrs Grant and I shared a bottle of white wine.

Wally seemed to feel that a eulogy was called for. 'He was a grand boss, your uncle,' he said. 'He could be strict, mind. But, when the work was done right, we got along fine.' He saw me glance in Alec's direction. 'But the youngster's a' right,' he added. 'We'll deal together.'

'He won't have a quarter of your practical experience,' I said.

'That's what I'm there for,' Wally said. 'In the old days, the farmer had to turn his hand to everything, from cutting and laying a hedge to being midwife to the beasts.'

'Agriculture had hardly changed in hundreds of years. But now,' Mrs Grant said, 'the farmer's a businessman. He – or she – does the paperwork and has the final word when decisions are needed. Unless it's a family business with everybody pulling their weight, it can be a mistake to pennypinch on before-tax labour. If the farmer tries to do a day's work on the farm and save a man's wages, he's doing the paperwork at midnight.'

'That's about it,' Wally said, nodding sagely. 'There's been times I've wished I had my own farm, but when I think of the forms to be filled, accounts to be checked and the quotas and allocations and . . . and a' that-like, I ken I'm happy enough on my tractor.'

'You're wise,' Mrs Grant said. 'I like to get up on a tractor myself now and again, but what with grants and subsidies and the

66

farm accounts . . . And there are harder times coming. The days when we could be sure of selling all we could grow have gone for ever. We've got to start looking for alternative land-uses, like sport. I'm replanting some of the trees and hedges I was given grants to take out.'

'So Mr Hatton said.' Wally paused. 'It was strange, him being ended that way.'

'Nothing strange about it,' Mrs Grant said sharply. 'We'd all warned him about shooting a gun which was out of proof. For myself, I made sure I was always two places away from him when he was shooting, and I noticed that Neil McDonald felt the same. I even bought him a set of hand-tools for loading, but he said he'd enough forms to fill in already without chivvying the police for a permit to buy black powder.' She switched her frown to me. 'What's that man Calder saying about it now?'

'Not a lot,' I said. 'He's in hospital. Car smash.' There was nothing to be made from her expression so I said, 'Nobody could possibly have tampered with his cartridges that morning, could they?'

'Nobody gave him any cartridges, if that's what you mean,' she said. 'Not in my sight. And he wasn't in the habit of leaving his cartridge-belt lying around. As far as I remember, he did as he always did, buckled his belt on before he got out of the car.'

'He never had any loose ones in his pocket?' I asked, remembering Keith.

'No, never.'

'And there couldn't have been a substitution at the house?' For the sake of peace I tried to make it a statement as much as a question.

Wally's mouth was full of the roast beef but he washed it down with a gulp of beer. 'No' at the farmhouse,' he said firmly. 'Mr Hatton was careless wi' locks – the most of us are, in the country – but yon Miss Nicholson's another body a'together. And she's seldom away from the place.'

'That's the ginger-headed woman at your cousin's table,' Mrs Grant said.

I stole a look and was reminded that no woman is ever quite fair to another. Alice Nicholson was only on the verge of transmuting from girl to woman (a change often quite unrelated to virginity or

67

to real age) and had the fragile look which brings out the protector in men and the claws in other women. Her hair was not ginger but a dark copper.

Wally continued as if uninterrupted. 'And, foreby, my wee house is just across from the farmhouse; the wife's aye home if I'm not and my old collie barks his head off at the fall of a leaf.'

'That's true,' Mrs Grant said. 'I don't know how you thole the beast.'

'I like a dog wi' a good loud bowf,' Wally said placidly. 'The burl of the tractors has done my hearing no good.'

I wanted to ask whether there had been any recent guests at the farmhouse but Mrs Grant might well have felt that the question was aimed at her. Wally saved me the embarrassment by slapping his knee.

'Hover a blink now!' he said. 'I've minded the last time I saw him. Ten days back, that was. Just before he went off to his other house, I spoke wi' him at his garage while Miss Nicholson and her friend were fetching out his special basket to him. I gied him the quote from Agrepair for sorting the big tractor and he took it wi' him to think about.

'The doos had fairly taken over the drying-shed for their nests and he wasn't wanting them fouling the new grain. So we'd spent the morn, off and on, me chasing them out for him to shoot until his belt was empty. He dropped the empty belt into his hamper and took a few boxes of cartridges out of his cupboard and tossed them after it. New boxes they were. There now!'

'That seems to settle that,' Mrs Grant said. 'If there was any tampering done, it was at Tansy House.' Her tone suggested that I could put that in my pipe and smoke it. She seemed quite unaware that she had changed sides in the argument.

'You're probably right,' I said. 'That seems to rule out Kirkton Mains Farm. Did my uncle's carelessness about locks extend to car doors?'

'Not a bit of it,' Wally said. 'He was usually careless the other way, locking the keys inside. It gets to be a habit, to click the latch as you get out. See, there was usually things in the car or the Land-Rover, like luggage or money or his guns, and you ken how folk are these days.'

We made noises of agreement.

Wally had finished his lunch. He got to his feet and made a stiff little bow to Mrs Grant. 'I'll just have a word wi' the new Mr Hatton,' he said, 'and then I'm away.' He nodded to me and left us.

'Do we know whether my uncle had any visitors at Tansy House during his last stay there?' I asked.

'He had me,' Mrs Grant said. 'As a guest, I mean. I was always welcome to his spare room whenever he was there,' she added, with delicate emphasis. 'I kept some things there against emergencies.'

'There's a frock in the wardrobe,' I said. 'I'll get it back to you.'

'I'd be grateful; I paid a mint for that dress. Anyway, nobody came near us and if we went out he left his dog in charge of the place.'

'Another good watchdog?'

'Boss is only a labrador,' she said. 'They're soft lumps. Even so, he has a strong sense of territory. I wouldn't want to try to slip past him ... if I were a stranger. Of course, he knows me well.'

'There were no signs of a break-in?'

She was silent for so long that I thought she had taken my question for a statement, but she was pondering. 'I don't think so,' she said at last. 'I always made sure that he locked up, but those sash-and-case windows are easy meat for a burglar. There was one occasion when we'd been out and Boss was behaving as if he was confused or uncertain about something. But he's a real glutton, like all labs, and I decided that he'd pinched something that you or I wouldn't think of as food and he wasn't sure whether to act guilty or not. That was on the Sunday afternoon, I remember.'

I wondered who had known that they would be out. 'Where had you been?' I asked.

'Just into Newton Lauder for a drink at the hotel.'

'On a Sunday afternoon?' My recollections of Scotland were still of a place where they padlocked the children's swings on the Sabbath.

She laughed. Her mellifluous voice produced an infectious laugh and I could see what Uncle George had seen in her. 'You're long out of date,' she said. 'We're quite civilised now up here. They re-wrote the licensing laws years ago. The pubs can stay open all afternoon if they want to, and all day Sunday.'

My cousin came over to join us but Mrs Grant decided that it was time she went. Alec saw her to the door and came back. He was looking harassed.

'Problems,' he said. 'Have another drink. I've got to rush off now. This is the time of year when farmers suddenly realise that the old harvester won't do another season. I've just had a call to Kelso relayed from the office. The offer of a bed still stands if you want it.'

'If I take another drink, I'll have to accept the bed,' I said.

'No trouble. Have it anyway.' He waved to the waiter. 'But I'm in a hurry. I gave Alice Nicholson a lift here. Could you take her back?'

'Of course.'

'The other problem is Uncle George's dog.'

'Boss?'

'Oh, you know. The thing is, he'd be welcome to a home at Kirkton Mains but I have three Jack Russells and they don't get on with him.'

'Who or what are Jack Russells?' I asked.

'Terriers. He's a lovely dog but he's unsettled and miserable and I can't find a home for him. I think he'd be all right in a place that he knows. Unless you take him, he'll have to be put down.'

'I don't know that I'm in a position to take on a dog,' I said.

'Well, will you at least meet him and think it over?'

'That much I can do.'

'Splendid. It's not so much a question of whether you take to him as whether he takes to you; he's been choosy since Uncle died. Now, I'll just make you known to Miss Nicholson.' He craned his neck to look around the room. 'She's vanished, damn it! Probably gone to the quine's shunkie. The ladies',' he explained when I looked blank. 'You wait outside and I'll bring her to you.'

I finished my drink and went outside. I took a seat on a bench in the sun and nodded and smiled as half-known faces went past. The funeral party was breaking up.

'Got a match?' A man was standing over me, a well-built man but with a squashed-down head and cold eyes. I had Uncle

70

George's gas pipe-lighter in one pocket and I produced it, but he shook his head angrily. 'Will Neil McDonald be long?' he asked.

'He was on his feet when I came out,' I said.

He picked a match out of the gutter, sharpened it with a small penknife and picked at his teeth. 'I'm a building worker to trade,' he said suddenly. 'Ian Yates. But Neil's been using me as his driver lately.'

I nodded. 'Since his tumble off the scaffolding,' I said.

'That's right. Since his tumble off the scaffolding.' He turned away.

Alec re-appeared with Miss Nicholson and I stood up. Her handshake was warm, dry and soothing.

'And now,' Alec said, 'the other most important introduction. Sit down again so that he doesn't feel threatened.' He turned to a car which I had not realised was his and opened a door. A glossy black dog descended. I knew very little about dogs but even I could tell that this one was a looker, and he walked with the kind of grace which eighteenth-century artists sometimes managed to depict in horses. He lifted his lip at a pair of passing legs, then came straight to me and sniffed my hand. I patted his head. And, as if that were introduction enough, he tried to climb into my lap.

'He likes you,' Alec said. 'Another problem bites the dust. You can take him back to the farm with you and home tomorrow.'

'On my motorbike?'

Alec looked harassed again. 'Oh, Christ! I didn't realise ... Miss Nicholson may not like ...'

Miss Nicholson had been looking sad to suit the occasion but now she produced a faint smile. 'I've nothing against motor-bikes,' she said. 'I was brought up with them.'

'That's all right then. I'll tell you what,' Alec said. 'Problems are for solving. I'll take Boss along with me now and leave him with your friends, the Calders, for you to collect tomorrow. And a bag of kennel meal.'

He whisked the dog into his car and took off.

'I never said I'd take the bloody dog,' I protested.

'I don't think he'd have heard you if you'd told him you were going to eat Boss for your Christmas dinner,' Miss Nicholson said. 'He has a lot on his mind just now.'

★

Alice Nicholson had the gift of silence. She walked demurely at my side, up the hill back to the churchyard. My uncle's grave had already been filled and the many flowers arranged over the bare earth. Cars still lined the roadside.

We stopped beside my Yamaha. 'You're sure you don't mind?' I asked. 'The breathalyser might not agree, but I'm fit to drive.'

Again the uncertain smile. 'I'm looking forward to it,' she said. 'As long as you don't go too fast.'

In honour of her fragile looks I insisted on her wearing my crash helmet. She stuffed a smart beret into her pocket and complied. I rode with a wary eye out for police-cars but saw no sign of them.

She directed me from the pillion, holding tight to my waist. I was very much aware of a pair of generous breasts against my back and her thighs against my buttocks, and I thought that she was not unaware of those pressures. Her skirt was tight so that she had to show a lot of slender leg but she seemed unconcerned. A few miles over minor country roads brought us to a farmhouse, by no means small but dwarfed by the barns in the background.

We stowed the Yamaha in a double garage between a battered Land-Rover and a red Mini. The metal doors looked across a huge concrete yard to a smaller house which, from the noise of the barking dog, I took to be Wally Ritchie's. She led me inside and showed me where to stow my small bag.

'Now,' she said, 'you'll not be wanting to eat again just yet. There'll be a meal about seven if that suits. Meantime, while I get the place sorted, would you like to take the dogs a walk? The poor devils have been shut up since first thing.'

'I'll do that,' I said. 'And then I'd like to take some photographs. Inside and out, if that's all right. For souvenirs.'

'Go anywhere you want,' she said.

The three terriers were in a small yard of their own with an attached kennel which still had Boss's name over the door. They seemed glad enough to be taken a walk, even by a stranger. While they hunted rabbits unsuccessfully through hedgerows and patches of rough ground, I took photographs. I kept coming across corners which, when I scaled them up, stirred my childhood memory, but I had quite forgotten the sweep of view across fields in full cultivation and miles of shining water. A mile away, near the shore and more towards Edinburgh, I saw a large industrial complex which I was sure was new to me.

Back at the house, with the dogs kennelled, I kept out of Miss Nicholson's way and concentrated on photographing every inch of the interior, as instructed. The zoom lens on the camera which Molly had lent me had too narrow an angle for interiors, so I took each room a section at a time. Molly had provided me with a dozen cassettes of film and I used nearly all of them.

This had been my uncle's principal home and, as was only to be expected, it was in the better state. The decoration was light and fresh and much of the furniture was new and good. Older or outmoded furnishings had been disposed of or banished to Tansy House to serve another turn. I sighed wistfully over some of the better pieces.

There was a fair-sized office with an electronic typewriter and a row of filing cabinets, the papers all, as far as I could see, relating to the day-by-day management of the farm. If there was a desk diary, the police must have removed it.

In the garage, there was a bench with a better set of tools than at Tansy House, although I had seen a still more fully equipped farm workshop among the barns. The garage bench was heaped with materials for his stick-making and several sticks, finished or in train. The metal doors were sturdy. Miss Nicholson took the key of the metal cupboard from the dresser, with no more comment than a slightly raised eyebrow, but it contained only a few boxes of cartridges (two of them with the name of Keith's shop on them), a spare cartridge-belt empty of cartridges and what I took to be the appropriate cleaning gear for a pair of twelve-bore shotguns. There were no signs that anything, doors or windows or the steel cupboard, had ever been forced open.

All this photography, and the changing of films in an unfamiliar camera, had taken time. I was vaguely aware that the light was fading because the light-meter was dictating ever-increasing apertures, but it took me by surprise when Miss Nicholson called to warn me that the meal would be on the table in ten minutes.

On my way to wash I looked into a small dining room. She had set a single place at the table. I put my head into the larger kitchen and saw another place set there. I told her that if she didn't fancy the dining room I would be perfectly happy in the kitchen with her. She made a token protest, but when I came downstairs again both places were set in the kitchen. It was by far the cheeriest room in the house, well lit and gay with colours.

She opened an indifferent wine – 'Mr Hatton's orders' - and accepted a glass. The dish was trout, exquisitely cooked with, I think, grated walnuts.

She had the features of one who could bubble with gaiety and the same personality came over from what she had made of a once gloomy kitchen. But although she was prepared to chat, there was a shadow over her which was not just bereavement or deference to the bereaved.

Into the conversation I worked the questions with which Keith had primed me. She was quite certain that the house could never have been entered – she was too fussy about keys for that. When I asked about my uncle's shooting cronies she looked at me seriously, with eyes which I saw were green. And I noticed that she had the beautiful skin which so often goes with that combination of eyes and hair.

'You're looking into his death, aren't you?' I was developing an ear for the many shades of accent. Some of them grated on me but I found hers charming.

'I wouldn't say that I was looking into it,' I said carefully. 'I'd just like to satisfy myself that there was nothing wrong with the sheriff's decision.'

'You'll not manage that,' she said. 'Yon mannie Calder had the right of it. I've not the least idea what happened myself but I grew up on a farm – near Kirkcaldy that was – and I've been around guns most of my life. I mind that one of my cousins – the daftest one of the bunch – used to use an old Damascus hammer-gun. It had never been as good a gun as Mr Hatton's and it was in a far worse state, and nothing would satisfy him but to go after the geese with magnum cartridges he could only just cram into the barrels. We told him he was glaikit, but would he listen?'

'I don't suppose so,' I said.

'You'd be right. And, even so, it held together for him for years until one day he was coming back over the foreshore, hurrying to keep ahead of the tide and with two greylags over his shoulder and the gun loaded. Well, I told you he was daft. Sure enough, he slipped and his barrels were two feet into the mud before the gun went off, which are about the worst conditions you could think of.'

'And even so the barrels didn't burst?'

'They burst all right,' she said, as if that were a matter of no account. 'It unravelled them like knitting. But nothing like the damage that I'm told was done to your uncle's gun, and my cousin was very little hurt and deserved all he got.' She stopped and looked at me through those green eyes, waiting.

I switched away from that hypnotic gaze and refilled our glasses. 'You think that my uncle's death was ... arranged?' I asked.

'I didn't say that and I'd hate to think it. He wasn't a man that gave folk cause to hate him. But it's hard to think that such a thing could be an accident.'

'Mr Calder tells me that it's commonplace for people to hand out cartridges, borrow them or whatever. "Here, try a couple of these." That sort of thing.'

She thought, pursing lips which I saw were full and delicately carved. I was beginning to see her features instead of accepting an overall impression. So far I could find no faults.

'Not your uncle,' she said at last. 'He might hand out a cartridge or two, but he wasn't one to borrow. He aye made sure that his belt was full and that he had a spare box with him. He said that he knew exactly how his gun shot with his favourite brand and he never did well if he made a change.'

'But there were two different kinds in the cupboard,' I objected.

'They're the same. Your Mr Calder has his name printed on the cartridges he sells, and he has his own box printed, but they're the same cartridge.'

It was my turn to pause for thought. 'Suppose somebody held out a couple of cartridges to him and said, "Here, take these. They're your usual brand and I've never shot well with them." Wouldn't he have taken them?'

'I suppose he might. You think that's what was done?'

'It's possible,' I said. 'And, if so, there's another possibility. It could be that the lethal cartridge was meant for somebody else and had been slipped into his belt but he passed it on to my uncle.'

75

She nodded slowly. 'I could easier believe that it was meant for one of the others,' she said.

'Can you tell me about them?'

'Yes. In a moment,' she said. 'There's a pudding.' She changed the plates. I would never for a moment have chosen rhubarb crumble for a sweet course but hers, with fresh cream, was fit for the gods.

'Now,' she said. But instead of telling me about my uncle's companions, she looked at me over her spoon and asked, 'Why do you wear that beard? It doesn't match your hair. And I know it's not that you don't have a chin, because there's one of your books on your uncle's shelf, with a picture of you before you grew it. Did some girl tell you that it suited you?'

'Lots of girls,' I said. 'Were they joking?'

She looked at me again with her head tilted. 'Perhaps not,' she said.

'Well, the real reason is that when I'm at the intense phase of writing I forget about everything else. I often forget to shave. After I'd found myself, for the tenth time, walking around looking fit to make children wake up screaming, I decided to let it grow. I was getting to be thought of as an eccentric. Whereas, if I forget to trim my beard it doesn't show for days. Does that make me a slob?'

'Not really,' she said. 'About your uncle's friends, I only know what I picked up from serving them a meal now and again, or from the men staying a night here. I never thought that they were good enough company for him.'

That surprised me. They had seemed a respectable enough group. 'Tell me,' I said.

'Where would you like me to begin?'

'How about . . . Mrs Grant?'

She sniffed disdainfully and lifted her small nose. 'She was the reason your uncle never married,' she said. 'Their affair started before I ever came here; before even her husband died, so they say. I can't tell you much about her, because I wasn't having any such goings-on here or folk might have thought that I was the same sort of woman. I told your uncle that if she stayed the night here she'd stay in the spare room all night or he could find another housekeeper. He laughed and called me mim. Prudish, you know? But she never came again, not to stay overnight. And she had to live with her neighbours and didn't want him staying there. So he was glad to keep on Tansy House when your aunt died. I didn't mind that. It was nothing to me what he got up to away from here. Men are men.'

The revelation that Miss Nicholson had not, after all, been one of my uncle's mistresses pleased me irrationally. And I rather liked to think of Tansy House as a love-nest. I believe that atmosphere can cling to a place and Tansy House had seemed happy; certainly not as prim and disapproving as one might expect from a Scottish Victorian villa.

'Why did they never marry, do you think?' I asked.

'She loses the farm if she marries again, and she likes fine to be the boss. She'd not have taken to coming here and being no more than a farmer's wife. What else do you want to know?'

An experienced investigator would have had a thousand more questions but my mind had gone blank on the subject of Mrs Grant. 'Let's move on,' I said. 'Hector Duffus.'

'Old,' she said. 'But well preserved. He still drives himself. Not very clean – I hated to change his sheets after he'd stayed here – but harmless enough in his old age. By reputation, he's not a man to be trusted in a business deal. And he'd been a devil for women in his younger days.'

'How would you know a thing like that?' I asked.

'Once, when he was here, he was taking a good dram, though he isn't usually as big a drinker as the others. He said that his youngest bastard had just passed twenty-one and so he didn't have to pay out any more.'

That seemed fairly conclusive. 'Is he married?' I asked.

'He brought his wife over once. A dowdy woman almost as old as himself and nervous of him. She'd have been scared to say a word, any time that he was trailing a wing. There's a son somewhere, a legitimate one, but I think he's abroad.'

'And Jim Fergus?'

'Mr Fergus's wife died a few years back. He was aye a drinker but he's got worse since then, the sort of drinking a man does when he's depressed and feels alone and needs company. It was his doing that your uncle lost his licence. Mr Fergus was already banned for life. Sometimes his daughter drives him here – she's fat and silly and married to a smallholder nearby. Another time he'll get a lift from Mr Duffus or Mr McDonald. They all live within a few miles of each other.'

'And when he's off the drink?' I asked.

'Then he's a harmless enough body and keeps his hands to himself, which is more than you could say for some. Shy, perhaps. But that's not often. Or maybe I see him at his worst. I mean, the times he's away from the farm for a day's shooting are likely the times he'll take to the drink, although I will say for him that he has the sense not to take more than a wee sup before the shooting's over. But, after that, you'd think that the world's supplies of barley bree were running out.'

'And Neil McDonald?'

She thought about Mr McDonald for a few seconds and a frown marred the perfect skin of her forehead. 'He's not married as far as I know,' she said. 'He can hold his drink and I can't say he's ever treated me without respect.'

'And yet you don't like him?'

'It shows, does it? No, I can't thole him but I couldn't tell you why. I just think that he's the worst of the bunch. Secretive. Most folk want to tell you about themselves, but not him. He never gives away a thing, just sits quiet and makes ill-hearted remarks between times.' She stopped and looked at me. 'That's not enough reason for misliking somebody, is it?'

'I don't think one needs reasons,' I said. '"I like him" or "I don't like him" are final and unarguable.'

'And that's just the way it is,' she said. 'I have the feeling that there's a temper, a passion, maybe the devil himself hiding inside there, but I could never tell you why I feel it.'

We fell silent again. I looked up at the ceiling to avoid falling forward and drowning in those eyes. 'He's a builder, somebody said. The others have farms to shoot over. How does he manage to give them a return invitation?'

'He rents a bit of Forestry Commission land,' she said. 'Quite a hantle of ground, I believe, though he's only in a small way of business. His firm's done building jobs around the farms, that's how they knew him. He was aye needing paid up as the job went along. I mind your uncle getting on at him once, asking him how he could be so short of a bit of working capital when he could run a big car and rent his bit of shooting. "Those men of yours are robbing you blind," he said. And Mr McDonald said that he knew to the penny what the men were getting away with and he'd soon put a stop to it if it went over the odds.'

She seemed to have run out of comments and I had run out of questions for the moment. She began to gather the dishes. I got up to help and it seemed natural to join her at the sink. As we did the washing-up in companionable silence another of Keith's questions came back to me.

'Do any of them have any particular friends or associates that you'd remember?' I asked.

'If they do, they never brought them here,' she said. 'Except for . . .'

'Yes?'

'There was one time, about two months back, I took the dogs and walked down the fields a bit to pull a cabbage for the lunch. I heard a shot from the rough ground among the wee woods near the march to the north-east.'

'What's a "march"?' I asked. It's not a word which you hear often in London.

'The boundary. So I walked on down and there was Mr McDonald, not looking a bit pleased to see me. He was with another lad, a younger man. They told me that Mr Hatton had said it would be all right, and Mr Hatton said the same thing himself later.

'Mr McDonald was very polite and introduced the younger man to me. He said that he was his nephew, John McDonald. But I'm sure I remembered him from school, although he'd not remember me, being a few years older so that I was only in a junior class when he left. But he wasn't John McDonald then. Hugh Ramsay, that's who he was.'

'Very odd,' I said. 'But you do get lookalikes. How sure are you?'

She shrugged. 'There'd been a lot of years between,' she said. 'And there's more than one chiel has freckles and a snub nose and sticking-out ears.'

When all was tidy we moved through to the living room. The night air was cooling the house and she lit a small fire. There was nothing to watch on the television but I found some soft music on the radio and pulled her up to me. We moved slowly around the floor in perfect accord, close but not pressed together, friendly strangers, sometimes talking, often not. The music finished and we sat again, together on the couch.

There was a question which I could not postpone any longer. 'What is it that's troubling you?' I asked. 'You keep retiring into some inner world. It may be none of my business but . . . It isn't just my uncle's death?'

She breathed in until I thought that she would burst. And then I saw the tears coming and thought that I had opened my big mouth once too often.

When a woman cries she will usually turn away; but Alice Nicholson turned towards me as a child does when she senses a comforter and the next thing I knew was that she was sobbing against my chest. I put my arms round her as I would around a weeping infant and wondered what the hell to do next.

'I'm sorry,' she said, several times, and when she had regained control she borrowed my handkerchief and dried her eyes but without pulling away. 'It's just all got a bit much.'

'What has?' I asked.

'Your uncle's death came on top of another – a girl I'd known most of my life was killed. I think she was my only real friend. And then your uncle . . . And your cousin has a girl of his own and plans to get married.'

'I didn't know that,' I said.

'She's abroad for the moment, but now that he has this place and an assured future they'll be wanting to marry and move in here and she'll not want another young woman about the place.'

'You may be wrong,' I said.

'Mr Hatton's already told me as much. And I've no other home and no family. But I'm just being silly,' she said sternly although the occasional sob was still shaking her slight frame. 'There's other jobs. I've little enough saved but your uncle left me a wee bit. I'll get by. It's just the thought of having nowhere to go.'

A weeping woman can be repellent but somehow Alice Nicholson's tears seemed only to underline her apparent fragility. It was not unpleasant having a girl to cuddle again and, as any other man would have done, I soothed her with words and strokes and little kisses until her tears had stopped but the kisses went on.

As we went up the stairs, still linked, I wondered what was expected of me and what I expected of myself. I had no wish to assume too much, nor to take advantage. To me, she had been a dependent creature. To her, had I been protector or just an animated handkerchief? Could such a strong, animal attraction be entirely one-sided?

She answered my unspoken questions indirectly. 'I put clean sheets on the spare bed. Did I waste my effort?'

I picked her up in my arms, like a child or a bride. 'That depends, doesn't it?'

For the first time, she stunned me by smiling, a blazing smile. 'I think my bed's the softer one,' she said.

From my earlier prowling I thought that I knew the layout. I carried her tenderly into the airing cupboard.

She made me breakfast in the morning. When I had my leathers on and was astride the 'bike I wondered what to say. She did not seem to expect protestations of undying love. I thought that agricultural communities were probably not over-awed by the facts of life.

'If you find yourself homeless,' I said, 'come to me. I couldn't pay a wage just now, but you'd be welcome to a bed while you looked around.'

She gave me a quick peck on the chin, which was all that she could reach under my visor. 'If I get stuck,' she said. 'Or if I find I'm pregnant.'

I rode off with the last word still loud in my ears. It was another word which is seldom heard these days, in London.

# EIGHT

If I had ridden home before visiting the Calders, I could have saved somebody an age of misery. But we had slept late and dallied again and I had detoured as instructed to leave the films with a laboratory at Penicuik, and now it was already afternoon and I wanted to enquire after Keith and to meet afresh the addition to my household.

So I turned off the Newton Lauder road and parked the 'bike outside Briesland House. I was stripping off my leathers when Molly, who had heard the 'bike arrive, opened the door.

'How's the patient?' I enquired.

She curled a lip and cast her eyes upwards. 'Go and ask him yourself,' she said.

'He's home already?'

'Against the doctors' advice, but he made such a nuisance of himself that they were glad to see the back of him.'

She sent me round the corner of the house to where, beyond an opening in the tall hedge, I found Keith established in a sheltered corner of the garden, making the most of the sunshine which seemed to have become a feature of that unusual year. He was comfortably settled with one plastered leg up on a stool and a table beside him cluttered with books and beer and a telephone. He was showing several dramatic bruises which had not developed when I saw him previously.

Boss, my prospective companion, was lying curled up with a large and shaggy spaniel beside a bowl of water, but at my approach he got up and loped forward to jump up against me.

'Squeeze his paw whenever he does that,' Keith advised. 'Do it hard. It's the only cure.' He indicated one of the other garden chairs.

I sat down. Boss tried again to climb into my lap. 'I'll remember,' I said. 'But it's unlikely that I'll be keeping him.'

'Whyever not? He's a beautiful dog. Your cousin dropped him off last night.'

'Yes. I'm sorry about that,' I said. 'I couldn't stop him.'

'Nothing to be sorry about. He was no trouble. Settled down with Herbert as if they'd been pups together. They've been fed, so you needn't bother again today. Why mayn't you keep him?' He lifted a beer-glass enquiringly and I nodded acceptance and thanks.

'In all likelihood,' I said, 'I'll be going back to London, to a small flat about a mile from the nearest park and my only transport a motorbike. You wouldn't wish that sort of life on him, would you?'

'I wouldn't wish it on you either,' he pointed out. 'What happens to him if you go back?'

'I look for somebody else to take him.'

'Failing which?'

I made a downward gesture with my thumb.

'That seems a pity,' Keith said, 'when he's taken to you.'

Boss was still climbing on me. I pushed him down and accepted the glass of beer. 'I think it's my uncle's suit that he recognises,' I said. 'And his soap and aftershave and toothpaste.'

'Perhaps. There may be more to it than that. They've little reasoning power but we tend to underestimate the power of their senses.'

I had put down the absence of his usual cheerful grin to his injuries, but they seemed to be bothering him so little that there had to be something else. 'Is everything all right?' I asked.

He started to evade my question and then decided to open up. 'Trouble brewing,' he said. 'Just what I feared. One of my recent clients consulted Duncan Cameron whose opinion, as usual, was diametrically opposite to mine. I've had a writ. Unfortunately, he lives near Linlithgow, so there's a fifty–fifty chance of it coming up before Sheriff Dougall.'

'That doesn't sound too good,' was all I could find to say.

'It isn't. It could be the start of a minor landslide. So let's see if we can't do something towards reversing the previous bad press. Tell me everything that happened at your end.'

I gave him a detailed account of my experiences since the ambulance had hauled him away, omitting only my lovemaking with Alice Nicholson although I think that he guessed it from my placid reaction to his news. He listened with a still intensity which I found disconcerting.

When I had finished – rather lamely, in view of my omissions – he thought for a moment and then asked, 'Did you drop off the films at Penicuik?'

'We can pick the prints up on Monday,' I said.

'On your way back from Knoweheid Farm. Duffus said we could see the place, remember, and I can't bend this leg to get into a car.'

'But . . .'

'Deborah can go with you,' he said firmly. 'She'll know what to look for. Who was the man the dog snarled at outside the pub?'

'I've no idea,' I said weakly. 'I was too interested in watching the dog. There was a Saab parked further along and I think the man got into that.'

'Quite right,' he said. 'Always watch the dog. He can tell you a whole lot more than you can see for yourself. Nobody's ever been able to work out for sure how much stronger a dog's power of smell is than a man's, but a thousand times is a reasonable guess. When you were clearing up at Tansy House the other day, did you go through with the vacuum cleaner?'

I stared at him, looking, I suppose, like an idiot. 'I did,' I said. 'But what's that got to do with anything?'

'What you've told me,' he said patiently, 'suggests very strongly that, if there was a substitution of cartridges, it was done at Tansy House. But the necessary tools to re-crimp a cartridge were also there. If somebody was going to enter and swap cartridges, why not do the tampering there as well? But shot is easy to drop and damned difficult to pick up again. When you Hoovered the study, did you hear a plinking sound?'

'I did. Would that have been lead shot?'

'I expect so,' he said. 'Were there any other signs?'

'What sort of signs?'

'I could guess, but I'd rather you remembered for yourself. Think, now. Did everything that you saw seem to have a rational explanation?'

'Good God, no!' I snorted. 'Look round any house and you'll

find odds and ends, broken bits of this and that, which nobody but the occupants could explain. I haven't thrown them out yet. I'll bring you over a carton to look through.'

He nodded, not at all put out. 'Don't forget whatever's left in the waste-paper baskets,' he said.

His words triggered my memory. 'There was something in the bottom of the waste-basket in the study,' I said. 'A half-moon of cardboard. Not even a half-moon, more the shape of a fingernail paring. Was that the sort of thing?'

The grin came back at last, all over his face. 'You see what you can do when you try!' he said. 'We'll make a detective of you yet. Did you find the piece of cardboard it had been cut out of?'

I thought back. 'No,' I said. 'But there was a flap missing from one of the cardboard boxes I was using to collect things in. Does it mean something?'

He was still grinning. 'Yes,' he said.

'What?'

'That's exactly the way to talk to him,' Deborah said. She came out of the french windows behind her father, carrying with some difficulty a tray loaded with several pistols and boxes of ammunition. 'He'll go on being all mysterious and enigmatic until you challenge him.'

'Well, I'm challenging him,' I said.

Keith threw up his hands. 'I'll tell you,' he said. 'It just seems such a waste of time explaining things. It seemed to me that, whoever he was, he'd know that his effort and the risks he'd taken would be in vain if anything about the cartridge was noticeably different after his work on it. So he'd want to put the shot back, to equalise the weight and so that it would rattle. Even a factory-loaded cartridge usually has enough looseness to let the shot rattle. If he'd substituted a solid or a plastic explosive for the propellant powder, he would have solved one problem. Another powder would be easier to fit into the case, but then he'd have to separate it from the shot so that it wouldn't mix through and possibly even start drifting out of the crimp. A proper cartridge has a thick wad to cushion the shock and to seal off the gases, but he wouldn't want to give up some of his space for the explosive. So he'd probably use a card wad. And if he cut it out on the spot . . .'

'He'd have to trim it to size,' I finished for him.

'Exactly. He carried away the rest of the piece of cardboard but missed the small trimming.'

'And now that that's settled,' Deborah said, 'let's get down to a little shooting.'

'You take too much on yourself, my girl,' Keith said severely. 'We haven't finished.'

Deborah was quite unabashed. 'All right,' she said. 'What did you still want to say?'

Keith scratched his ear. 'Until we get the analysis back, I'm not sure that there is anything more to be said.'

'Yes, there is,' I said. 'Why did you expect, or want, my uncle to have some shot in him?'

'Oh, that! I thought it was obvious. Somebody could have been careless among the rabbits and shot him dead. So they could have faked a different accident to cover up the negligence. But apparently not. Now, Deborah. Fetch the target frame and set it up against the wall and we'll do a little shooting.'

For the next hour Keith sat at ease, occasionally taking a shot from his chair at the rank of targets or demonstrating some point about loading or handling. But for the most part he was happy to watch benevolently while leaving me at the mercy of his daughter.

That young lady was a protracted explosion of information. She knew her facts. In her view I needed to know them. And I was going to be force-fed with them or we would both die in the attempt. She was also an extremely competent shot. Under a bombardment of instruction I fired automatic pistols, revolvers both single and double action and, just for the sake of variety, the occasional shotgun or rifle, from every position short of standing on my head, until I felt that I was achieving, if not skill, at least a modest competence.

Molly at last gained me a respite by bringing out a tray of afternoon tea. (She also made me feel like a fumbling amateur by casually picking up a large revolver and hitting a swinging can six times from the hip.) By that time I was exhausted and, despite the ear-protectors, going deaf, and my mouth was foul with the taste of gunsmoke. But I had also decided that my next thriller would contain real guns . . . and a dedication.

We had finished our scones and were sipping the last of the tea when Keith looked up and said, 'Trust a Highlander to smell when the kettle's on.'

A uniformed superintendent of police was approaching from the front of the house. He was a bony, gangling man with a long face set in lines of despondency (although Keith told me later that he had once heard the superintendent laugh). He seemed to be known to the family. Molly gathered up the tea-tray and departed to make room. I stood to be introduced to Superintendent Munro.

'What brings you out this way?' Keith asked. 'My accident? Or have the neighbours been complaining about our shooting on the Sabbath?'

'Your neighbours are beyond earshot, as you very well know,' the superintendent pointed out, 'and some target-practice by a certificate holder on his own premises is neither here nor there. The matter of your accident I will happily leave to my men, in the hope that justice may be done. No, I came, for once, to seek your advice.'

His tone made it clear that he wished to speak with Keith alone. Deborah wanted to take me off to the coach-house to hear how shots indoors differed from those heard outside, but Keith stopped her. His left wrist was taped, but he managed one-handed to check that each pistol was unloaded, and while he did so he spoke to Munro.

'Is it anything which Mr Parbitter shouldn't hear?' he asked. 'If there's any running around to do while I'm laid up, he's doing it.'

Munro weighed me with a glance. 'You can keep a confidence?'

'Without any difficulty,' I said.

'What I've to say is not for publication, not without I say so. You understand?' And without waiting for an answer, he went on. 'I have your book about the McSween case. There was a small error about police procedures, but it was a competent job. When next you want information about police organisation in Scotland, telephone me.'

Scotland, it seemed, was full of critics. But helpful critics.

Keith snapped the cylinder back into the last revolver. 'Right,' he told Deborah. 'Take them upstairs and clean them.'

'You could have trusted me,' she said coldly.

'I know I could, Toots. But there's no harm being doubly safe.

Any time I've done the checking I won't resent it if you check again.'

She gave her father a relieved smile, picked up the heavy tray and vanished through the French windows. Keith's eyes followed her. So, I must admit, did mine. That girl was developing a walk which would turn heads within a year or two.

When I returned my attention to Munro, I saw that the superintendent was looking embarrassed.

'I am in some difficulty,' he said to Keith. 'While I know exactly what you will reply I do not yet know what I am going to say.' I looked at him but he was perfectly serious.

'Tell me what I'm going to reply, then,' Keith said. 'That may be a start.'

'Very well. You will say what you have said in the past, that the police are against private ownership of guns and are trying to reduce the numbers in private hands by making it difficult and expensive for the individual to buy or keep them. You will tell me, for the twentieth time, that the Firearms Act permits but does not require us to inspect the ground on which a rifle is to be used and that we do so only to inflate the costs of the system and of the issue of a certificate, and so to ration their ownership by cost and bureaucratic inertia – I think that those were your very words – all of which I will deny with my dying breath. And you will go on to say that the controls over the private citizen are administered by officers who often know less about firearms than the citizens concerned.'

Keith was grinning. 'All right. I've said all that. What am I replying to?'

'You have not finished yet,' Munro said severely. 'You will say that the citizen has a right to protect himself and that if he waits for the police to come to his aid he is likely to receive too little help and too late. You will go on – because you always do go on – to point to the instances when a trained police officer has shot an innocent person and to suggest that such cases outnumber the accidents occurring with firearms in private hands.'

The superintendent paused for a deep breath before resuming. 'You will probably add that firearms should be kept out of police hands and that the military should be called on when armed force is needed.'

Keith's grin had vanished. 'Would I be wrong?' he asked.

'That is neither here nor there. You will only have dragged it in as an irrelevancy and because you can never resist the grinding of axes. You will also say that I have a bloody nerve – because you use that sort of language – asking for your help when one of my officers is in deep trouble over the use of a firearm.'

'And what will you say to that?'

'I shall apologise for having wasted both our times.' Munro moved as if to get up.

Keith laughed briefly. 'You devious old Hebridean bastard!' he said. 'You know that I can't say any of those things now that you've said them for me. You're talking about the aftermath of the robbery at Haliott Castle?'

'I am,' Munro said, settling back in the garden chair. He saw that I was baffled. 'You did not hear about it?'

'Scottish news gets very little coverage in the English media,' Keith said. 'It was the week before your uncle's death. I only know what was in the Scottish papers and you can't trust a reporter to get more than his own name right, if that. Tell us about it, Munro.'

'Very well. Haliott Castle, you must understand, is nearer Edinburgh but falls within the Borders Region and my Division.'

'It isn't a proper castle,' Keith put in. 'More of an old fortified farmhouse.'

'Aye, that is so. And fortified it may have been,' Munro said, 'but fortifications are no protection if folks will open their doors to a knock late at night. Lord Haliott was at home, with his family and three servants.'

'There's no Lord Haliott,' Keith said irritably.

Munro looked surprised and mildly shocked. 'That is how he is always known.'

'Not by me. He's Donald Farquhar who used to own the chain-stores. There was a Victorian convention that the owners of certain properties could style themselves "Lord", but the Lyon King of Arms would never recognise them and if they tried to take a seat in the House of Lords they'd be slung out on their ear. At the most, he's Farquhar of Haliott.'

Munro sighed and plodded on. 'Be that as it may, there were eight folk in the place when the gang of four arrived, armed with

89

three pistols and a sawn-off shotgun. The telephone line had already been cut. A manservant tried to make a fight of it and was killed, almost blown in half with the sawn-off shotgun. With that example before them, the remainder of the household did as they were told and were tied up and left on the floor of the hall.

'The robbers moved without haste and seldom spoke above a whisper. They knew exactly what they were looking for and where to find it. The folk were bound with unnecessary savagery and lay there all night until the grieve found them in the morning.'

'The grieve is the farm foreman,' Keith told me.

'Aye. One of the servant girls is in the hospital yet. The gang left with some paintings and other valuables and a large collection of jewellery belonging to the lady.' Munro paused, perhaps expecting Keith to tell him that the wife of Farquhar of Haliott was not a lady, before going on.

'They left no clue behind them and we had little to work on, although the MO suggested that this was the work of a gang which had carried out four other robberies in the past eighteen months. Next day, however, there was an anonymous 'phone-call to tell us that some of the men we wanted could be found at an address in Edinburgh.

'Because of the killing of the manservant, the Regional Crime Squad had been invoked; but we were acting in close liaison with them and one of my constables who had been first to enter the castle was acting as a scene-of-crime officer. It was no more than a matter of routine to send him to witness the arrests and to agree the list of any property recovered.'

Keith had been listening intently with his eyes, half-closed, looking vaguely at a distant treetop, but now he brought them back to Munro. 'The papers were giving his name as Allerdyce until the whole mess became *sub judice*,' he said. 'Would that be a youngish man, fair-haired, with an unusually gentle manner for a policeman?'

'It would,' Munro said.

Keith nodded. 'He was sent to do the routine comparison of guns in stock with the books. He seemed more open to reason, and even a wee bit more knowledgeable, than most of your men.'

'He'd been on the firearms course.'

'I know about that course,' Keith said. 'Once a week for six months he'd go and spend the day queueing for a gun, queueing for ammunition, queueing for a chance to shoot, about fifteen minutes – if he was lucky – in being told how to point the gun and damn-all about how to handle himself in action.'

The superintendent surprised me by nodding slowly. 'There is something in what you say,' he agreed. 'Be that as it may, although the Crime Squad was in charge they required the consent of at least an assistant chief constable of the local force before firearms could be issued. In my opinion, a handful of armed officers could have done the job, but the only available ACC is a cautious man and he would not give his consent without being satisfied that there were enough armed men present to conduct a full siege. Three men to go in, two cordons and a support unit.'

'That's a lot of men to assemble in a hurry,' Keith said. 'They'd have to scrape the bottom of the barrel.'

'They did. There was no doubt who would be the leader and his number two in entering the house, they were both experienced men who had done such work before. Other men of experience were needed to head the other teams. When it came to picking the third man for the raid, it emerged that my man was young, fit and recently trained and he was invited to volunteer, in terms which made refusal difficult if not impossible.

'The raid, you understand, was timed for three in the morning.

'Sledgehammers were available, but it had been decided to enter by stealth if possible in the hope of overcoming any resistance before it began. The front door was not bolted and the leader was able to slip the latch and cut the chain without arousing anyone in the house.

'Once inside, the leader and his number two checked the ground floor.

'My man, Allerdyce, was left to guard the stair. He took up a position near the top, from which he could see both floors. He heard sounds from the downstairs room but took it that the others were hunting for weapons. He described the scene to me and I can well imagine it. A house silent but for occasional sounds which might have come from below or above. Waiting, wondering who or what might come at him and whether he would move fast enough to save his own life.

'When it happened, it was with the suddenness of a mousetrap.

At one moment there was nothing. He heard a sound and there was a figure at the stairhead. He could make out few details in the dimness. He swears that he thought he saw a gun, but he may have imagined it, or be imagining it now, or be inventing it to justify his action, I just do not know. He swears that his revolver went off without his conscious volition. The person above him was thrown back against the wall, lived only long enough to say the word "Basket!" and then fell forward on top of him and they tumbled down the stairs together. When his colleagues pulled him out, the other was a girl and she was stone dead.'

Munro paused as if uncertain how to proceed.

'Are you being mealy-mouthed?' Keith asked. 'Did she really say "Bastard!"?'

'"Basket!" is what Allerdyce said to me.'

'He may have been pandering to your delicate Highland ears,' Keith said. 'I would definitely have said something stronger if I'd been an innocent bystander and a nervous copper had put a fatal hole through me. But never mind. Was a gun found?'

'A man was discovered hiding in the bedroom and in a drawer there was an automatic pistol with his fingerprints all over it. Also a sawn-off shotgun and a supply of cartridges – with your shop's name on them. That, unfortunately, is all.'

'What size of shot in the cartridges?' Keith asked.

'Nobody has seen fit to tell me that,' Munro said. 'If it matters, I will try to find out. It has been suggested, on Allerdyce's behalf, that the girl might have been carrying that pistol and that the man might have had time to retrieve and hide it, although he denies taking any such action.

'The depute chief constable held an enquiry and he has reported to the procurator fiscal, who recommended that Constable Allerdyce stand trial for manslaughter.'

Keith's eyes snapped wide open. 'That's unheard-of, isn't it?'

'On the mainland, it is unique,' Munro said. 'But the team leader and his partner swear that they had cautioned Allerdyce because he seemed over-eager to draw blood. He denies that absolutely.'

'And you want me . . .?'

'To help the defence to prove that a nervous young officer who was expecting to be confronted by an armed and desperate robber might well let off a shot without conscious intent, and hit his . . .'

'Target?' Keith suggested softly.

'There was no target. Let us just say that he hit the person who startled him.'

'So I would expect,' said Keith. 'A handgun is designed, and the user is trained, so that the bullet should strike wherever he is looking.'

'You would speak to that?'

'I would. Now let's take it a point at a time. Had he cocked his revolver?'

'He says not.'

'Have him think carefully. Under the Guidelines, he would have been entitled to cock it. He believed that a confrontation with a person armed with a lethal weapon was imminent.'

'The Guidelines are confidential,' Munro said hotly. 'How did you get sight of them?'

'You really want to know?'

'On second thoughts, no, I do not. And I have just taken the trouble to refresh my memory of the wording. He should have had grounds for believing the confrontation to be imminent. Grounds. Does the cocking of the revolver make much difference?'

'About ten pounds of difference to the trigger-pull – if the revolver was properly adjusted. Could you get your hands on it, for me to examine?'

Munro rubbed his head and then shook it. 'I will try, but I think it unlikely at this stage. It will certainly be produced at the trial.'

'Make sure that it isn't tampered with,' Keith said. 'And try to get test-pull figures for it, cocked and uncocked.' He glanced at me out of the corner of his eye and I thought that I could see an amused twist to his lip. 'Would it help if I could find at least one person who had let off a shot unintentionally while nervous and startled?'

I felt myself blanch.

'Aye, it would,' Munro said. 'Can you do that?'

'One at least. But don't build your case on it. The trigger-pulls would be very different . . . unless the revolver was already cocked. I would be surprised, myself, if a young and inexperienced officer, tense and waiting, did not cock it.' I had the feeling that Keith was dropping a strong hint to be passed along the line.

Munro started nodding and checked himself. 'What else?' he asked.

'Could you get to question the man who was found in the house?'

Munro shook his head impatiently. 'If he removed and hid the gun to make things easier for himself he's unlikely to change his story now, although it may be worth a try.'

'Were any of the stolen goods recovered?'

'A few items were found hidden in the house, and one or two from previous robberies, but only trifles and none of the jewellery.' Munro frowned at Keith. 'I do not see the connection.'

'Perhaps you prefer not to see it,' Keith said. 'Why are the two other officers so hostile? And what were they doing while Allerdyce waited on the stair? Surely the proper drill would have been to get on with searching the rest of the house.'

'That is how I would have done it,' Munro said. 'But the leader has discretion.'

'Did he use his discretion to have a hunt for the missing jewellery on his own account? And did he find it? And is his hostility to Allerdyce intended to draw attention away from himself? Get the officer in charge to give his estimate of the time from entry to the sound of the shot.'

Munro sat silent for a full minute, his eyes locked with Keith's. 'I have been told to stay away from the witnesses,' he said. 'I supposed that it was in case I might try to influence them.'

'Allerdyce's lawyers could ask for the opportunity to take a statement from the prisoner,' Keith said. 'Or we might look for a friend of the man, to visit him in prison and . . . drop hints. The sort of hints I wouldn't even want to say aloud,' he added quickly. 'And you might just have the word put about among any known receivers that any products of the robbery are too hot to handle, even if brought in by a police officer.'

Munro sighed deeply. 'It will be a sad day for the police if that idea comes to anything and a worse day for Allerdyce if it does not. I shall see what can be done. What else?'

'I'll go through my library in search of parallel cases,' Keith said. He smiled wryly. 'That's all I'm fit for at the moment. And it might be helpful if we found a psychologist who was working on behavioural responses, to speak on human reaction under stress.'

Munro pursed his lips.

'I know one of those,' I said. The other two, who had forgotten that I was there, looked at me as if I had dropped out of a tree. 'On my way north, I stayed the night with a friend in Newcastle. Derek Onslow. He's a lecturer in psychology. You can find several of his books in the public library, if you want to check up on him. Shall I ring him? He was talking about coming up for a few days. It's the vacation just now.'

Keith nodded. 'Do that,' he said. 'Do it now.'

I went into the house and used the study 'phone. Derek Onslow was at home and would be glad of a few days in the country and away from his more demanding colleagues. 'Would Monday suit?' he asked.

'I'll be away that day,' I said. 'Make it Tuesday.'

I returned to the garden. Munro was looking more cheerful. 'I am happier in my mind,' he was saying, 'now that I know that something is moving. But I notice that you have not mentioned a fee for your help. Either the fairies have replaced you with a changeling or you want to put me under an obligation. What is it that you want?'

'Nothing very much,' Keith said.

'What not very much?'

'I'd like some help to get at the statistics on crime and firearms.'

'But they are published annually,' Munro said.

'In a form carefully designed to obscure the issues. I want to see the figures before they are lumped into misleading categories. For instance, I want to isolate offences committed with legally held firearms. And I want to compare the number of innocent bystanders shot by criminals with the number shot by the police.'

Munro stiffened. 'You only wish to write another article to make us look like idiots,' he said.

'You don't know that,' Keith said. 'I might wish to press for better training in firearms for police officers, over an assault course.'

'And pigs might fly,' the superintendent said bitterly. 'But you have my promise. Young Allerdyce counts for more than our public image.'

He paused. The pairs of eyes were locked together. 'I will answer the question which you have not yet asked,' Munro said suddenly. 'I am becoming skilled at anticipating you. No, there has not yet been a reward offered.'

'There will be,' Keith said.

# NINE

Acting as depute to Keith during his convalescence, and with Boss frisking beside me, I saw the superintendent to his car. The warmth was going out of the day. When I returned, Keith was looking less unhappy, almost pleased with himself. 'Help me inside with my bits and pieces,' he said. 'Time for a drink before guests arrive.'

'Guests?'

'We usually have guests at weekends. It's good for Deborah to learn how to comport herself in polite society. Not to fart while a guest's speaking, that sort of thing.'

I gave him his crutches and picked his books and papers off the table. We moved into the study. I poured drinks for both of us, carried a gin and tonic and a diluted white wine to where Molly and Deborah were working in the kitchen, and came back.

'You don't really expect me to give evidence, do you?' I asked him.

'Why not?'

'My lack of a shotgun certificate, for one thing.'

'Apply for one straight away. Your accidental discharge didn't happen until next week. And remind me to give you some more cartridges before you go.'

I was none too keen to stand up in court and admit my folly, but Keith seemed to regard the matter as settled. 'Who's coming to dinner?' I asked incuriously. 'Anybody I know?'

'You know Ralph Enterkin. The other will be Sir Peter Hay.'

It took a few seconds for the name to hit me and then I took a much needed gulp of my whisky. 'I think perhaps I'd better go,' I said.

'Why, for God's sake?'

'He came to see me a couple of days ago. He put my back up.'

'Peter did? That doesn't sound like him,' Keith said. 'He's a very well-liked old boy.'

'I was feeling a bit hungover and leftish,' I explained, 'and he seemed to be implying that he had some right to shoot over my bit of land. Morally, perhaps he had the right. But I feel safe on my own ground. I like to think that wild creatures are safe there too.'

'Those pheasants aren't exactly wild,' Keith explained without heat. 'They owe their existence to the fact that Peter put them there for that purpose.'

'Even so. I'm afraid that I was rude. And a bit stupid.' I summarised my talk with Sir Peter. My attitude sounded even less rational than how I remembered it.

Keith took a sip and thought about it. 'Well,' he said at last, 'I wish you hadn't. Peter's a fine man and he's been a damn good friend to this family. And to most of the locals, come to that. Also I'd hoped to borrow a spare Land-Rover off him for your running around, until I can get the car replaced or repaired. But I dare say he'll just look on it as the ignorance of the English city-dweller plus the eccentricity of the writer.'

I wondered whether to cringe or to let my hackles rise. 'I don't want anybody to make allowances for me,' I said. 'I'd better go.'

'You'll have to face him some time,' Keith pointed out.

'Not necessarily. I may decide not to stay.'

He shrugged. The idea that somebody might voluntarily return to London was beyond him.

We had not heard the Rover arrive nor the sound of the doorbell, but suddenly Deborah was ushering Mr Enterkin into the room. We shook hands politely and I explained that I was just leaving.

'Then I'll walk to your car with you,' he said. 'I came early in the hope of a word with you on neutral ground.'

'On Sir Peter's behalf?' I asked.

'Of course.'

'For Heaven's sake stop circling like a couple of dogs disputing territory,' Keith said. 'Give Ralph a drink, Simon, top up your

98

own glass and both sit down. Neither of you has anything to say that you can't say in front of me.'

'We could surprise you,' Enterkin said with a trace of his usual twinkle, but he accepted a seat and a stiff malt. When he looked at me, the twinkle was gone again. 'Sir Peter has told me of your discussion.'

'And Simon has told me,' Keith said. 'He feels that he may have been hasty.'

'Sir Peter feels that he may have tried to rush you, causing a certain understandable reaction.'

'That's very gracious of him,' I said. 'But I spoke out of principle.'

Enterkin sighed heavily. 'You are both my clients, so it seemed incumbent on me to mediate before the matter gets out of hand.'

'How much further could it go?'

'A long way. Sir Peter has spent time and trouble, relying on your uncle's promise.'

'I do know that,' I said.

'You may not know that Sir Peter is also the superior of your feu.'

'You told me that I didn't have to pay any feu duty,' I protested.

'You don't. Recent legislation made it possible to redeem feu duty by a single payment and your uncle took advantage of it. But that did not change the other conditions on which you have the land. I attempted to outline the position the other day, but you cut me short.'

Enterkin leaned back and sipped his drink. I had the impression, despite the severity of his expression, that he was enjoying himself. 'Nowadays,' he said, 'feu charters are concerned with such matters as the superior's rights to prevent undesirable constructions on the land. Customarily, the superior is given the right to take back the land, and any buildings thereon, if any building or alteration work is carried out without his permission. We now note, to our surprise, that two windows have been added, and a porch, without any reference being made to your superior. Of course, the more stringent terms in the charter are not usually enforced . . .'

'But in this case, Sir Peter intends to make an exception?'

99

'Certainly not.' Mr Enterkin sounded shocked. 'Feu charters often contain survivals of earlier days, when the conditions were sometimes quite whimsical. A snowball from the north face of Bennachie was an example, as was the presentation of a rosebud in May. But originally the reasons for feuhold tenure were exactly what you would suppose. Feudal.

'The feu charter of Tansy House,' he continued, 'seems to have been copied without amendment from the charter pertaining to an earlier dwelling on the site. And that may have derived from one of even earlier date, although I have so far been unable to trace it further back than the seventeenth century. It contains an absolute requirement that the occupier, whenever the superior has need of him, shall raise six men at arms and come to the service of his overlord.'

Keith shouted with laughter. I was less amused. 'But there's no war at the moment,' I said.

'And,' said Keith, 'when war breaks out between our two countries – as it may very well do, one of these days, if Westminster goes on as it's going – Simon and his men-at-arms will likely turn up on the other side.'

'The charter,' Enterkin resumed solemnly, 'says nothing about war, but about need. If your acres remain as a hole in the middle of Sir Peter's shoot, he will have great need of extra beaters in order to work round them.'

'You mean,' I said, 'that I have to send six beaters every time Sir Peter wants to shoot?'

'Not send. Bring. Your presence is required. Unless you would care to accept a rental and allow arrangements to continue as before. Two pounds an acre is the customary rent for sporting rights, is it not, Keith?'

Keith controlled his laughter. 'In the special circumstances, I'm sure Peter could go to three quid an acre,' he said.

'No,' I said firmly. They both looked at me. 'I need the money. But I don't want it. I told Keith earlier that I liked to feel that wild things on my land were safe. Maybe I can't hold to that. But I don't want to feel that I sold them.'

'Very understandable,' Enterkin said. 'Perhaps I might 'phone Sir Peter now, Keith. To avert embarrassment, he also was prepared to abstain from the pleasure of your table.' The twinkle

100

was definitely back in his eyes when he turned them to me. 'I think you'll find that your differences are quite forgotten.'

I had my doubts, but Sir Peter must have had a more forgiving nature than mine because his attitude, when he arrived, was friendly and quite without triumph. Over dinner, his first concern was for Keith's injuries but, once he was satisfied that these were, if not trivial, at least temporary, he turned his mind unasked to the matter of transport.

Keith said that the family could manage with the Japanese jeep, his shooting vehicle, while the car was missing, but that I was committed to visiting Knoweheid Farm on the Monday.

'But I can do that by motorbike,' I said.

'Leaving your dog shut in all day,' Sir Peter said. 'I understand that Boss has been tacked on to your legacy. Got to think of him now. I came here in the spare Land-Rover. I'll leave it for you. Ralph can run me home.'

'God's blessing on you, noble benefactor,' Keith said lightly. 'I want Deborah to go along with Simon on Monday. She'll have a better idea of what to look for. And I'm not having her going around on pillions. Especially if some nut's running potential investigators off the road.'

'And I want somebody else to go along with them,' Molly said.

'Oh, Mum!' Deborah said. 'We don't need a gooseberry.'

'I never thought you did,' Molly said placidly. 'Could Ronnie be spared?'

'I have a meeting on Monday,' Sir Peter said wistfully, 'or I could have gone along as chaperon cum bodyguard. Yes, take Ronnie along. He's got the roe under control down here and he needn't be up north for another week.'

I felt that I was being bulldozed. With the others in common agreement it was hardly for the stranger in their midst to object, but I did point out that Ronnie had a Land-Rover of his own.

They all laughed at that. 'You can't have seen inside the back of Ronnie's Land-Rover,' Sir Peter said. 'Take mine. I've vehicles and to spare until the season comes in.' He gave me a shrewd glance from under his ragged eyebrows. 'Apart from having the knack of it,' he said, 'what makes a young fellow like you go in for the writing as a career? The search for immortality?'

'Hardly that,' I said. 'It's good to leave something semi-permanent behind. But somebody once said that Heaven is being remembered with affection. Sometimes I have a mental picture of dying and being met by one of my characters.'

'Julian Dawson?' Sir Peter suggested.

I cocked an eyebrow at him. I had not expected him to be among my readers. 'That's very perceptive,' I remarked. '"But, I say, "you're not real." "I'm more real than you are," he says. "You'll fade away, but people remember me."'

The others laughed but Deborah gave a little shiver. 'Are you writing anything just now?' she asked.

'At the moment, I seem to have written myself out. Except . . . I've been chewing at one idea but I can't quite make it work.'

'Tell us,' Sir Peter said. 'We might have thoughts.'

I hesitated. Discussing my work in prospect always seems like exposing myself in public. But the whisky had loosened my tongue. And he was right, they might have ideas.

'Imagine a rich man,' I said. 'He's old and he has a terminal disease. He goes to a top clinic. After all the tests are done, the head man explains to him why his condition's inoperable. "The body," he says, "is an enormously complicated machine, and when disease has progressed as far as yours the repairs are quite beyond our technology. But," he says, "we do have a simpler technique. It's expensive."

'"Tell me," says the rich man.

'"We call it the Whole Body Transplant," says the head of the clinic, "although that's a rather upside-down way of looking at it. Complicated as the body is, the sense of personal identity is housed in a small lobe of the brain, perhaps the easiest organ of all to transplant. We can put you, in the sense of being yourself, into another body."

'"But what body?" the rich man asks.

'"We can't do everything for you," says the head of the clinic. "That's for you to solve. You go and find a volunteer. Some handsome, healthy and vigorous young man who's tired of life. Or who has money troubles but wants to leave his loved ones provided for. You leave a will dividing your money between him and his loved ones, and the two of you come in here together. The old, sick shell fails to survive but you, as an identity, awake in a new, healthy and rich body."

102

'"Could it really be done?" asks the rich man. "Do such volunteers exist?"

'"It's done quite often," says the head of the clinic. "Can't you think of any rich young man who seemed to appear suddenly on the scene with no evident past?"

'The rich man thinks and he can remember several such men. And, almost the next day, he bumps into a handsome and virile young man – or woman, if he prefers – who is talking about suicide.'

There was a momentary silence round the table. 'I thought he might,' Deborah said.

'Now we come to the difficult bit,' I said. 'The rich man suspects that it's a confidence trick, but he has no wish to leave his money to his own family, whom he dislikes. He decides that he has nothing to lose. He goes ahead. The question is, does he think it's a con but it turns out to be for real, or vice versa?'

'It would be a confidence trick,' Enterkin said, 'set up by the rich man's own family.'

'How can you be so sure?'

'Only a family would pull a trick like that. I speak from the depths of my professional experience. And it would have to be a trick because, while you might be able to transplant the ego, memory would remain behind unless you transplanted the whole brain. There would be no point in surviving as an individual without that individual's memory.'

'Yes, there would!' Deborah shouted.

'Really, Toots!' Keith said reprovingly.

'Sorry,' Deborah said more calmly. 'But listen. Suppose the idea was that he could adopt an unwanted baby, leave his money to it and then go into the clinic with it, knowing that he had another whole life coming with his money intact.'

'I like it!' Sir Peter said. 'Simon, where is this clinic? I must go and put my name down.'

'And then,' said Enterkin, 'his family could challenge the will.'

'And the lawyers end up with all the money,' Keith suggested.

'Of course,' the solicitor said cheerfully. 'We all love a happy ending.'

The motorbike went into one of the Calders' sheds for the moment. I tried to put Boss into the back of the Land-Rover, but he kept jumping over into the front until I gave up. His head, which kept finding its way onto my knee, got in the way of the gear lever and made adjustment to driving the heavy vehicle in the dark more difficult.

At Tansy House, I pulled off the road and stopped in front of the garage. If I were stuck with a dog I would need four-wheeled transport. The 'bike was valuable, but it might not trade in for much of a car. I shook myself. What was I thinking? I was enjoying myself, but this was not my country.

Boss knew where he was and descended from the Land-Rover with a soft bark of pleasure. He paused to empty his bladder, which I thought was probably to mark his territory, but as we approached the door I heard his small sounds change from relief to anxiety. It was a long time since I had had close company with a dog, but I could read the signs and I wished that I had the walking-stick gun with me.

I told myself that I was imagining things, that Boss had expected to find his real master here and was disappointed, no more, at finding the place dark. But when my key turned the latch I pushed the door and stood to one side.

Nothing came out. The house seemed silent.

Boss slipped past me. I heard him growl once and then go up the stairs in a hurry. He whined, on a note which puzzled me. But it was not, I thought, the sound of a dog which has found an intruder. Not a live intruder.

I found the switch and lights came on in the hall and stair. The place had been a mess but surely it had been a more orderly mess than this?

It had been searched.

I started to look around, but Boss whined again from the head of the stairs. My bowels felt loose. I would have liked to visit the bathroom but somebody or something might be awaiting me there.

The walking-stick gun was still in the hall stand, which was a double relief. It might have to be my cushion against insolvency while I wrote another book but I would be sad to part with it. Apart from being a beautiful artefact, it inspired the holder with confidence. Perhaps with misplaced confidence, I reminded myself. I loaded it with one of the replacement cartridges which

Keith had given me and went up the stairs, keeping my finger carefully clear of the trigger.

But for that precaution I would undoubtedly have let off another shot.

A woman was lying on my bed. Her ankles were bound and her hands were tied behind her back. There was a gaudy splash of dark red at her face and across the coverlet. I could not see properly because Boss had jumped onto the bed and was licking at her face. I felt sickness in my throat.

Fighting down the urge to run screaming from the house, I took one more look.

The red was a long scarf which had been tied twice around her head, once across her eyes and once between her teeth. She was still moving, trying to keep her face out of the way of that intrusive tongue.

Panic receded and then returned. What to do, quickly before somebody arrived and found me in that compromising position? 'Phone for the police? Cut her loose? Suppose – my God! – suppose she were to accuse me of raping her!

I got a grip on myself, turfed Boss off the bed and untied the scarf. I could always put it back if she started screaming.

She had difficulty making a sound. She worked her jaw and eventually some saliva returned to her mouth.

'You will be Mr Parbitter, no doubt?' she croaked matter-of-factly.

I said that I was.

'I'm Mrs Beattie,' she said, as if that explained everything.

It took me some minutes to free her, because the knots in the nylon had been pulled very tight. I fetched the carving-knife and cut it and then she needed time to get herself moving again. She bit her lip as sensation came back. As soon as she could stand she insisted on being helped, with Boss in fussy attendance, down to the kitchen where she seemed to feel more at home, and while she massaged her limbs I made her some tea. She was a plump and doughy-faced woman in her late thirties, with tight curls which gave her a doll-like look.

At last her story began to come out.

Mrs Beattie lived on a small farm about a mile along the road and had been in my uncle's occasional employment, cooking and cleaning for him when he was in residence and keeping an eye on Tansy House when he was away.

'I heard that you was here,' she said. 'My man saw the lights on. I meant to ask whether you wanted me to do for you as I'd done for poor Mr Hatton.'

'I can't afford help at the moment,' I said.

'That's a shame. A laddie like yourself needs a woman about the place. My man went off to Edinburgh this morning, to the friendly. Hibs against Hearts,' she explained. 'So I just thought I'd walk along and ask. But there was no answer at the door, so I decided to come in and write a wee note.'

'The door was open?' I asked.

She shook her head without dislodging a curl. 'Your uncle aye left a key under the stone aside the front door, so I took it and let myself inside. I was hardly through the door when I was grabbed from behind and my scarf was round my face. I was helpless in his grasp. Helpless!' She seemed to relish the last word.

'There was only the one of him?' I asked.

'Only the one laid hands on me, but I think there was another because I heard whispering. He bundled me up the stairs and made me lie on your bed. When he pulled my tights off I thought I'd be raped, but no. He tied my hands with one end and my ankles with the other. Then he pulled my skirt down decent and left me. I heard him searching through the place a whilie longer and then he was gone.'

'We'd better call the police,' I said.

'Dinna' cry them out for my sake,' she said. 'I've no need of the fuss. My man's awfu' jealous.'

'I'll give you a run home,' I said, 'and then I'll look around. If anything's missing, I'll have to call them.'

She nodded and poured herself another cup of tea. Now that the excitement was over it was time to talk about it. 'You're a lovely speaker,' she said. 'It must have been a shock to you, finding the place a' tapsalteerie, and me on your bed like that.'

'By God it was!' I said.

She looked at me coyly. 'When you saw me there,' she said, 'what was the first thing you thought of doing? Be honest, now.'

'To be honest,' I said, 'I was tempted to load you into the back of the Land-Rover, just as you were, and dump you in the Square at Newton Lauder in the hope that you'd been abducted from somewhere else and didn't know where you'd been.'

I locked up carefully, removing the key from under the stone, and drove a rather subdued Mrs Beattie home. Then I 'phoned Keith. 'I've taken a quick look around,' I finished. 'Most of the house has been turned over, but the study and kitchen are tidy. So I think we can assume that he got what he wanted.'

'Not necessarily,' he said. I could almost hear that quick brain racing at the far end of the line. 'Look carefully at the kitchen and study and then call me back.' He hung up.

I examined the two rooms and saw what he meant. I called him back. 'You're right,' I told him. 'They've been searched, but carefully. What do you make of that?' Sometimes he made me feel stupid. I could have reached the same conclusions, but I needed more time.

'What I make is that he started on the kitchen and study. He was trying not to leave any traces. Then your Mrs Beattie came and walked in on him. Once he'd dealt with her, there was no chance of concealing his visit so he stopped bothering. And so, unless you know something you haven't told me, or unless he was being very subtle, he didn't find what he wanted. Is there much damage?'

I looked uncomprehendingly around the living room. 'One or two things broken,' I said. 'They look accidental, due to haste, not deliberate vandalism.'

'Cushions or upholstery slit?'

'No,' I said. 'Does that tell us something about what he was looking for?'

'That, or how it arrived there,' he said.

I waited but he did not expand the thought. 'Should I call the police?' I asked.

'Should, yes. Shall, that's up to you. I would suggest not. Don't throw away anything which has been in the house longer than you have, start a new bin-bag and one or more of us will come over tomorrow.'

Carrying the walking-stick gun, I walked Boss under a rising moon and then gave him a biscuit and put him into his bed. Clothes had been dumped all over the bedroom floor but a few minutes were enough to restore some sort of order. It had been a long and busy two days and a night. I slept like the dead.

# TEN

Boss woke me, at not too unreasonable an hour for a Sunday morning, with a demand to be let out into the garden. Keeping a dog seemed to bring with it a load of responsibilities. I had only a vague idea of what they were, but Boss knew all about them and was well able to keep me advised. He let me breakfast in peace but then, after reminding me to fill his water-dish, made it clear that he expected to be taken for a walk. I told him that I could see how he came by his name, although Keith explained later that he had been named after a famous gunmaker.

Just why Boss found my company essential to his morning constitutional was not revealed to me. After all, he knew the routine and his way around far better than I did. But I found that walking a dog on a fine morning while thinking random thoughts was an excellent way to start the day. We went out of the back door and walked down the neat and orderly garden, trying not to notice the ravages of pigeon and neglect. Fruit trees spilled shade. The grass was dotted with fallen apples and needed cutting. I looked in a wooden shed to find some tools including a heavy old mower.

We left the garden by way of a gate in the end wall. Boss looked at me enquiringly, then seemed to shrug his shoulders and led me by a well-trodden way round the edge of the small field and through the wood. I tend to fall in love with places rather than with people and the wood was a delightful place, a cathedral of shape and silence cared about by nobody but children and keepers. Beyond, the ground rose and we climbed a small valley. Pheasants scuttled ahead of us, irritated rather than frightened. They knew, and Boss knew, that they were out of season. My mind took note of the changing views, of patchwork fields and strips of wood and unfamiliar hills, while pursuing its own paths. I wanted to use the time to think about writing, but found myself thinking back to Uncle George. I remembered him as a man who meant to be kindly but had not always understood. Once, he had tried to show me how to skin a rabbit. While the head was wrapped in the everted skin it had looked like a dead baby. My distaste for shooting dated from that realisation.

For no reason, an explanation for one of Keith's questions jumped into my mind. If there had been any likelihood that my uncle had known of whatever was the object of the search, upholstery would certainly have been slit.

I found that we were back at the gate before my thoughts had ordered themselves. Several rabbits fled across the grass at our arrival and Boss, who had a strong sense of territory, chased them under the shed. I left the gate open so that they could get out again. Boss looked at me as if he did not understand.

The prospect of re-entering that disarranged and dusty house, either to tidy the invader's mess or to stare again at blank paper, was repellent. Instead, I got out the heavy mower for an assault on the grass. But my uncle must either have been very fit for his years or have had help about the garden, because I was sweating after the first line of cut and breathing like an asthmatic after the second, while the mower had doubled in weight and resistance. I was too stubborn to give up, but half-way down the grass for the third time I was glad to be interrupted when Deborah came through the gate beside the house, wheeling a push-bike.

'Hullo,' she said cheerily. 'Dad said to see if you wanted any help to clear up after your burglar. Nobody answered the front door.'

'I was just having a go at the grass,' I said feebly.

'So I see.' She looked at the mower with contempt. 'Well, even if I hadn't just cut all of ours – Dad being laid up and all that – I wouldn't lay a finger on that thing. It should be harnessed to a horse. If you want to do a bit more, I'll start tidying up inside. Or you can bring the Land-Rover across one of these days and collect me and our motor mower and I'll do it for you.'

That was too good an offer to be refused. And I preferred that anything picked up in the house should go where I could find it again. 'Hang on while I wrestle this monster back into the shed,' I said. 'How's Keith today?'

'He was going to get back to his workbench but Mum wouldn't let him, so he's sitting in the garden with a stack of books, newspapers and some scribbling paper.'

I thought about it and decided that that answered my question.

'Mostly they're old books of shooting memoirs,' she said, 'but there was one book entitled *Propellants and Explosives*, so we can guess what he's working at. He said to tell you that he's been on the 'phone and there's a reward offered for the Haliott jewellery. Ten per cent from the insurance company and another ten from Lord Haliott – or Donald Farquhar, Dad calls him.'

That seemed an odd piece of information to send me but I put it away in my mental filing system and forgot it.

We pottered away the rest of the morning pleasantly enough, with Uncle George's music-centre permeating the house with lightweight melodies. Tansy House began to look tidier than it ever had since my occupation. It was the second time I had sorted through the place and as order was restored I became sure that nothing was missing. For lunch, we shared the sausage rolls which I had intended for my evening meal.

Deborah decided to clean the kitchen although it looked pristine to me. I was wondering whether I would do more harm than good if I tried my hand at weeding the garden when I heard a car pull up outside. I went out. Molly was parking the family jeep on the patch of worn ground, too unkempt to be called a drive, which fronted the garage. In the back, Keith sprawled on a pile of cushions with his plastered leg sticking out over the tail-gate.

'We came to see how you're getting on,' he said, 'and maybe to give Deborah a lift home.'

'I told him he shouldn't be rattling around in cars yet,' Molly said, 'especially in bouncy ones like this, but he insisted and serve him right. Are we in the way?'

'Not a bit,' I said.

They came in with me, Keith managing nimbly on his crutches. I expected them to sit down and await tea like the usual run of formal visitors, but Molly joined Deborah in the kitchen. Keith clunked around, nosing into things.

111

'Have you emptied the Hoover-bag yet?' he asked.

I got out the vacuum-cleaner and we emptied its bag onto a newspaper. Keith produced a roll of freezer bags and detached one into which he started collecting tiny spheres. 'Number six shot,' he said. They could have been marijuana seeds for all I could tell, but he seemed to know what he was talking about.

He was starting the self-imposed and unsavoury task of sifting through the contents of the black polythene bin-bag when the doorbell rang. The smarter Land-Rover had appeared again and Sir Peter Hay was on the doorstep.

I took him in and gave him a chair. For the moment, we had the living room to ourselves.

'I called on impulse,' he said, 'but I seem to have chosen an evil hour. You have a full house.'

Deborah put her head in from the kitchen. 'Don't worry about us,' she said. 'Hullo!'

'Hullo, m'dear! Listen,' Sir Peter told me seriously, 'I've been thinking about that story of yours, the one you outlined last night. Couldn't get it out of my mind. Forget what Enterkin said about memory, the average reader wouldn't think of it. Make your rich man a shooting man. Base him on me, if you like, I wouldn't mind. Make your head chap at the clinic an opponent of bloodsports with a son who's a fanatic on the subject. The man your rich man meets who's willing to undergo the operation, he's the son putting on an act. You follow me?'

'So far,' I said. 'Or is that it?'

' 'Course it's not. The punch-line is that your rich man's almost sure the whole thing's a con, but he's dying anyway – he's had a dozen other opinions – so he decides to go through with it. Nothing to lose, see? And when he wakes up, he's got fur and whiskers, he's a rabbit on his own land and the keeper's after him with a gun. How do you like it?' Sir Peter asked anxiously.

At first glance it looked good. As happens to me once the idea has come, I could see ramifications proliferating to infinity, alliances and frictions, twists and contrasts, little philosophical messages. But, before I could say so, Keith humped himself into the room. 'Did you know that you'd left the garden gate open?' he asked.

I told him that I did. 'I let a few rabbits in while I was walking the dog this morning. I left it open so that they could get out again.'

'All their friends have joined them,' Keith said. 'They're hopping like fleas on a blanket out there. They'll clean you right out of vegetables in a couple of nights.' Having dropped his bombshell, he settled into a chair and lost interest. He dropped a carrier-bag beside his seat.

I closed my eyes for a second. There was always something.

Deborah popped out of the kitchen. 'I'll see how many of them I can chase out again. Come, Boss.' In his haste, Boss scooted the hearthrug under my chair.

'Shouldn't use a gundog to chase rabbits,' Sir Peter said. 'Bad for training.'

'I don't shoot,' I reminded him.

'Maybe not,' said Keith. 'But if anybody trustworthy wants to borrow him, let them. The only time a dog's really alive is when it's doing what it was bred and trained for.'

Sir Peter nodded sagely but evidently decided that the whole subject had been covered by those few words. 'How are you getting on with your two cases?' he asked.

Keith pulled a wad of paper from his pocket, a mixture of clippings, photocopies and notepaper. 'Making progress,' he said. He selected a photocopy of what seemed to be a page of a book. 'This was written during the supremacy of the hammer-gun. The author blandly assumes that all shooting is done with a pair of guns and a loader. It's from a chapter about safety. "It is sometimes the case that an eager Gun" – in this context, Gun means the man holding it – "prefers that his loader pass him the guns already cocked, thereby saving some fractions of a second when the birds are coming thick and fast, but this is not to be commended and should be discouraged by the head keeper. Only last year, it happened that an experienced Gun, whose practice this is or was and who should have known better, discharged his piece close by the ear of his loader. The loader, who was in the act of cocking the other gun with the barrels pointed to the ground (another unsatisfactory practice as has already been explained) allowed, in his startlement, the hammer to slip and shot dead the Gun's favourite dog, a piece of retribution which should prove a lesson to all save the unfortunate retriever."'

'The thumb isn't so likely to slip off the spur of the hammer if the muzzles are pointed skyward,' Sir Peter explained to me. 'But, Keith, that isn't exactly parallel.'

'I know it. But if you give a court a moment of amusement you get a more sympathetic hearing. Here's a better one, from the twenties. A man was shooting rabbits over ferrets. After a long wait for a rabbit to bolt he fired at the first sign of movement and shot the ferret. You can't say that that isn't parallel. The ferret was an innocent bystander.'

Deborah came back. Boss dropped, panting, at my feet. 'We got most of them out,' Deborah said, 'but some went under the shed. Can I use your 'phone?'

'Go ahead,' I said. The day was already beyond my control. I offered drinks. Keith and Sir Peter accepted beer. Uncle George's stock was becoming sadly depleted.

'Uncle Ronnie's coming over with a ferret,' Deborah announced on her way back to the kitchen. Keith and Sir Peter nodded, quite accepting this as the normal course of events.

Keith read out two more passages before the doorbell went again. 'Ronnie's been quick,' he said as I got up.

I expected Ronnie's large frame and rough-hewn face and his ragged Land-Rover, so that the delicate presence of Alice Nicholson on the doorstep and a red Mini in the road caused the feeling of unreality which had been growing all afternoon to burst into full flower. She could have been the original Alice in the Wonderland of Tansy House. I stepped back and she followed over the threshold.

'It's all right, isn't it?' she asked. She was almost tearful with anxiety again. 'Your cousin and his fiancée turned up yesterday, not long after you'd left. When she realised that he'd been staying in the house while I was there, she hit the ceiling.'

'I can see how she might,' I said feebly.

'Yes, well, there was the father and mother of a row and I said that I'd leave today. But I didn't have any money for a hotel – Mr Hatton said he'd send me a cheque when he could – and you didn't answer the 'phone last night and you'd said I could count on a bed if I was in any difficulty, and the Mini had a full tank . . .'

'It's all right,' I said. 'Calm down. Of course you're welcome to a bed.'

She had moved into the open living room doorway but she stopped dead. 'But you've got people in . . .'

Sir Peter had got to his feet but Keith sat tight, tapping his cast in explanation. 'If you're Miss Nicholson,' he said, 'I'm delighted to meet you.'

I performed introductions. Molly and Deborah came out of the kitchen. As she shook hands, the young devil winked at me. Trust a girl to detect the tiniest traces of a sexual relationship.

Alice gravitated to the kitchen as if to her natural habitat. She saw the cloths and basins. 'But I should do that,' she said.

'We were just finishing,' Deborah said. 'We've sloshed several pounds of guck down the drain. So at least you can start from scratch.'

The doorbell went again. This time it was Ronnie with a silvery ferret clinging to his shoulder. The feeling of unreality became stronger. Alice had gone round the kitchen in one quick rattle of slamming doors and drawers and came out to shake hands with Ronnie. She stroked the ferret, which was more than I would have dared to do. It was a beautiful little animal but it looked savage, like some women I had known not wisely but too well. Cuddlesome, but ready to draw blood.

'So where's these mappies?' Ronnie asked.

Alice drew me into the kitchen. 'Are we expected to feed all these people?' she whispered urgently.

'Nothing's been said,' I whispered back. 'I owe the Calders a couple of damn good meals. But there's nothing in the house. We'd better hint for them to go.'

She looked at me contemptuously and then glanced out of the kitchen window. 'There's vegetables and fruit in the garden. And meat.' When it came down to domestic instead of personal problems, she was calm and in control. 'Do you have any money?'

'Not much.' I handed over a tenner. The money which I had pocketed after the lunch following the enquiry had melted.

'Ample.' She checked the pans, found the pressure cooker and moved to the living-room door. Ronnie and Deborah were making a move towards the garden. 'Wait for me,' she said and, to the others, 'there'll be a meal in about an hour if somebody will go for a few ingredients. I saw a corner shop open as I left the town.'

'I'll go,' Molly said.

Matters seemed to be out of my hands again. I rejoined Keith and Sir Peter at the dead fireside. They were talking about dogs again.

I heard the ferreting party return. Deborah stayed in the kitchen with Alice but Ronnie joined the men, bringing his ferret with him, and accepted the last of the beer. Boss had returned to my side and seemed quite unconcerned when the ferret walked over him. The ferret – named Archie, Ronnie told me – climbed onto my knee. Greatly daring, I did as I was advised and stroked him. He settled down on my shoulder. I relaxed very slowly.

Keith reached out and poked Ronnie's arm. 'According to Mr Hatton's daily, he used to leave the key under a stone. Who'd have known that?'

'Aabody kenned it,' Ronnie said. 'Well, most. If he wanted a haunch of venison he'd 'phone me and say to put it in the freezer and there'd be money on the kitchen table. He did the same with most folks.'

'M'hm,' Keith said. He drummed his fingers on his cast. 'So. While Mr Hatton and his lady friend were out for a drink – on a Sunday, note – somebody entered this house. Somebody who knew about the key. Probably somebody known to the dog. He doctored a cartridge, spilling a little shot in the process – it's damnable stuff for spilling and you can't just wipe it up.'

'But he didn't search the place. He, or somebody else, entered yesterday. Somebody who knew about the key and knew that Simon would be away. He intended to leave no trace. He'd already put the key back under the stone, which allowed the unfortunate Mrs Beattie to walk in on him. It seems unlikely that he got what he wanted.'

He fell silent. We waited but he seemed lost in thought. 'Oh, come on,' I said. 'You can say a bit more than that about the two cases.'

Sir Peter gave a snort of laughter. 'He could, but he won't. I know Keith of old. He'll be miles ahead by now. But he never says what he's thinking until he's good and ready.'

'I don't know anything to say,' Keith said. 'I may make a few guesses. You can do the same. You know as much as I do,' he said, looking at me, 'and probably more. But one thing that you don't know, Simon, because the robbery and the arrest occurred while you were still in England, makes me think that we may not have two cases, we might just have the one.'

Sir Peter, Ronnie and I made surprised noises so that Boss looked up. Even Archie the ferret seemed to be taking an interest. When I moved my head a fraction I could see his little pink eyes glaring at Keith.

'What don't I know?' I asked.

Keith was still holding his wad of papers. He picked out a newspaper cutting and looked at it. 'The name of the young man who was arrested upstairs in Edinburgh. Hugh Ramsay.'

The name meant nothing to me at first. In my mind I ran over all that I had reported to Keith and it came back to me. My eyes went to the closed kitchen door. 'The man Alice Nicholson met with the builder, McDonald?'

'And who was going under a false name.'

'It's not a very direct link,' I said.

'I only said that we might have one case, not two. Might.'

I began to get up. 'Sit down,' Keith said. 'If you talk to a woman while she's cooking, your dinner burns. She can talk to you but not vice versa.'

'There's one urgent question,' I said, 'and it needs only two words to answer it.' I took the cutting out of his hand and took it into the kitchen. I was back within five seconds. 'I suppose you knew that Laura Kenzie, the girl who was shot, was the friend Alice Nicholson was so upset about.'

'I thought that she probably was,' Keith said. 'That's why I said that I was glad to see her. But we can ask a few very gentle questions over the meal.'

Ronnie and Sir Peter already knew some of what we had been discussing but they were bursting with questions. Keith filled in the missing facts for them but refused to be drawn into speculation. 'Time enough for theorising after we know what Miss Nicholson can tell us, and what's found at Knoweheid Farm tomorrow, and what Munro can find out for us. And what's in the lab report.'

Ronnie glared at him. 'I'll bet you ken fine what'll be in that lab report,' he said.

'I could guess,' Keith said blandly.

I thought that I might steal some of his thunder. 'You were reading up the subject this morning,' I said.

'Only to add a little confirmation to what I'd guessed earlier.'

'What, then?' Ronnie said gruffly.

'Do you know what's meant by a high explosive?' Keith asked me. 'As against any other kind.'

'No idea,' I said.

'All explosives burn rapidly – that's what an explosive is. Propellants, as in cartridges, are comparatively slow. High explosives simply burn much more quickly, almost instantaneously. That's why they're more powerful. I think that a high explosive was substituted for the propellant powder in one of your uncle's cartridges.'

'Tell us which,' Ronnie persisted.

'Picric acid, if you're so bloody desperate,' Keith said. 'Now, are you any the wiser?'

Molly came back and delivered a carrier-bag to the kitchen before joining us. Luckily, she only asked for a sherry and there was still some in the bottle. By the time an extra seat had been placed for her, the thread of the discussion had been broken.

Keith sat where he was and ate off a plate on his knee. The small dining-table accepted the rest of us, squeezed up into an intimate and friendly huddle. I had expected Sir Peter to hanker for greater formality but he seemed thoroughly at home.

As we sat down, Alice passed me far more change than I had expected. 'Mrs Calder insisted on buying the wine,' she said.

'But all this food . . . ' There was a pie on the table and vegetables, cheese and biscuits, and the table was set for a sweet course.

She laughed, woman triumphant, and began serving. 'Rabbits,' she said. 'I've put two more away in the freezer. Potatoes and carrots from the garden. Windfall apples and plums. Mushrooms from just beyond the garden wall. We only needed a better cheese, some ice cream, an onion and some respectable coffee. We'll have to start putting things away in the freezer, for later.'

'Well done,' I said humbly. We started on the pie. 'And well done Archie. This is delicious.'

'The rabbits could have done with hanging,' she said. 'But there wasn't time.'

'Archie only killed the once,' Ronnie said. 'The others were down to Miss Nicholson.'

Somehow I could not see Alice running fast enough to catch a rabbit. I paused in the act of opening wine. 'How?' I asked.

'I used your uncle's walking-stick gun. You don't mind?'

In the circumstances, I could hardly object.

'If you can hit a running rabbit with a four-ten stick-gun,' Keith said from behind me, 'you're good.'

'Mr Hatton always let me use it. I wouldn't have touched either of his twelve-bores. He rather liked the walking-stick gun himself. He could walk with it and be ready to collect a rabbit or get rid of a pest if the chance was there. I'd better give it a clean,' she said to me. 'Where have you put his gun-oil?'

'I don't know,' I said. 'The whole place has been re-arranged twice. What did it look like?'

'An aerosol. It would have been in his hamper of personal things. He was sure he was going to forget something if he was always packing and unpacking, so he kept a big basket packed with spares of everything. Clean clothes, pyjamas, spectacles, toiletries, notepaper, something to read. Anything he used out of it was replaced for next time.'

'I remember,' I said. 'I emptied the hamper and used it to collect the things I don't want but somebody else might. But any aerosols are on the shelf above the kitchen door.'

As the meal vanished and the wine went round, the atmosphere became progressively more festive. Ronnie, who had forsworn the wine but had captured the remains of Uncle George's whisky, lost his usually surly manner and produced a fund of scandalous tales about the local worthies.

Keith brought the party down to earth with the cheese and coffee. He asked Alice, out of the blue, 'Do you mind being asked about your friend who was killed? Laura Kenzie?'

'I've accepted it now,' she said sensibly. 'And these things are better talked about. That's why funerals are as they are.'

'How did you first hear about it?'

'It was on the television news.'

'That must have come as a shock.'

119

'It did,' she said. 'No warning at all, just "Here is the news." and bang! At least when Mr Hatton was killed somebody came and broke the news gently. But after hearing about Laura that way, it was days before I could open a paper or see the news, in case something else was going to jump out at me. Was that silly of me?'

Keith looked at me.

'Not in the least,' I said. 'Maybe you saved yourself another shock. You never saw the name of the man they arrested at the time Laura was killed?'

She shook her head, puzzled. I could see that she had braced herself for another blow.

'It was Hugh Ramsay. Probably the same Hugh Ramsay you told me about meeting near the boundary of the farm.'

She relaxed. Colour came back into her face and knuckles. 'Him!' she said. 'I couldn't think of anybody ... Hugh Ramsay can get himself arrested any time for all I'd care. He had a friend or two, at school, but mostly he was disliked. And feared. He was a bully. And the tricks he'd get up to sometimes with the young girls ... The police were at him more than once. I was too young to catch his attention, and was I thankful!' She looked round the table, meeting our respective eyes. A shy girl, she was beginning to enjoy being the centre of attention.

'Tell us as much as you can about Laura Kenzie,' Keith said. 'Was she pally with Hugh Ramsay?'

Alice refilled coffee-cups while she thought about it. 'Not especially, that I remember,' she said. 'At that age, I'd hardly notice the like of that. The most I could say would be that, as I mind, she was less afraid of him than the others her age were. Laura was older than I was, so that our paths rarely crossed.

'It was much later, in fact only last year, that I bumped into her in Edinburgh, in House of Fraser. We'd been speaking to each other about the price of clothes, the way one does when one meets up with a stranger, before we realised that we'd been at school together – she'd put on a little weight and taken to tinting her hair. So we went for coffee and we seemed to get along.

'She was a bit evasive about what she was doing and where she lived, and I didn't push it because I guessed that she was living with a man and lonely during the day. When she heard that I was out in the country and often on my own, she asked if she could come and see me. She took to coming out about once a week, swinging an old duffel-bag which usually had some food for our lunch. I told her it was silly, bringing food to a farm, but she said she didn't feel so much of a scrounger that way. I could understand that.

'She'd give me a hand to get finished up early, and we'd go for a walk or give the men a hand about the place. She got on fine with Mr Hatton and she was company for me. That's all I can think of except . . . that I got the impression that she was under somebody's thumb. When it came to time to leave, she seemed scared that she'd miss the bus. It was as if she had to be home before her man.'

'Could it have been that she was afraid of missing her lift?' Molly asked. 'If she was secretive about having a boyfriend, she might not have let on that she was being dropped and picked up.'

Alice thought it out while she buttered a biscuit and cut a sliver of cheese, very neatly. 'I think you're right,' she said at last. 'She never let me walk down to the road-end with her. And I did wonder, once or twice, what bus she could be catching.'

I looked over my shoulder. Keith was studying his newspaper clipping again. 'I see that Hugh Ramsay was described as a technician with Calchemco, whoever they may be. Are they out what used to be your way?'

Alice nodded and swallowed quickly. 'That's the big chemical complex just down the hill from Kirkton Mains Farm,' she said.

'But she never said anything about where she lived or who she lived with?' Keith persisted.

'Not a word.'

Keith drummed his fingers on his cast again, an irritating sound.

'I didn't think that burglars had jobs by day,' I said.

'Munro tells me that they're the most difficult to catch,' Keith said. 'The fuzz soon get to know a full-time crook who spends money without any visible income. But a man with a job or a small business, who turns to crime at night, can sometimes mystify them for years.' He returned his attention to Alice. 'Tell us about the last time you saw Mr Hatton,' he said. 'I know you told Simon, but go into it in more detail.'

Alice started to gather the dishes. 'Is all this really helping to clear up any mystery about Mr Hatton's death?' she asked at last.

'I hope so.'

'So do I.' Alice sighed deeply and shudderingly. 'Because that was the last day that I saw either of them. I think perhaps it was my last happy day. I owed him a lot. I surely owe help to anyone who's chasing whoever killed him. It just seems so remote, me keeping the house straight and waving him off, from somebody slinking around and planting a sort of bomb on him.

'He'd told me, the night before, that he was coming here for a few days. I supposed that he and Mrs Grant had found that they could both get away at the same time, that's how it usually was.

'Laura turned up that morning.'

'Unexpectedly?' I asked.

'A bit. She hadn't 'phoned or anything, but usually she didn't. She knew that she could come any time. I was surprised because she'd visited only a day or two earlier.'

We were all listening avidly. It was Deborah who asked the question. 'Did she seem as usual?'

'I remember her as being nervous,' Alice said slowly. 'But I could be making too much of it. She was an intense sort of person. Jumped at loud noises, looked into dark corners, that sort of thing. And she could be as sweet as pie one minute and then take offence at something somebody said and fly off the handle.

'That morning, we cleared up the kitchen together and then she did the Hoovering while I made the beds.'

'Could you hear the vacuum-cleaner moving around?' Keith asked. 'Or just droning?'

Alice shook her head in irritation. 'If you think that Laura put a doctored cartridge into Mr Hatton's belt, you couldn't be more wrong. I could hear the cleaner moving around. And, anyway, Mr Hatton had asked me for the key to his cupboard in the garage, that morning before she arrived. There was only one key and I usually had it for safekeeping. I kept it in a teapot on the dresser.

'While we did the housework, Mr Hatton had been clearing pigeon out of the drying-shed. About the time we finished, I heard Mr Hatton calling to me that he'd be leaving shortly. Up to then, Laura hadn't been out of my sight since she arrived, except when she was Hoovering. Satisfied?'

'That seems conclusive,' Keith said. 'Go on.'

'The one thing Mr Hatton liked help with was his hamper. He was getting on and he'd had one hernia, and it was an awkward lift for one person. Laura and I carried it into the garage for him. He was giving Wally his final instructions and at the same time he was filling his cartridge belt, which took the whole of a box of cartridges.

'He looked in the hamper and decided that he needed more cartridges with him. Laura was going to get another box or two out for him but he said no, he'd do it himself. So you see, she'd no chance to swap anything over. You do believe me?'

'You're very loyal,' Keith said, 'but we believe you.'

'Thank you. We lifted the hamper into the Land-Rover for him. He drove off. He 'phoned me that night and asked me to send on some papers. And that was all.'

'Yes. You do appreciate,' Keith said, 'that she was in the Edinburgh house with Hugh Ramsay and seems to have been living with him? And that he's awaiting trial for armed robbery?'

'I know that,' Alice said.

'I have the impression that you're not altogether surprised.'

'Well, I'm not. I said that we got on well, and that much is true. But there was aye something in her manner that my mother wouldn't have liked. I always felt that she disregarded questions of right and wrong except so far as they could rebound on her.'

'Yet my uncle liked her,' I said.

'Men are always disposed to like a girl,' Alice said. 'Another woman sees a trace of slyness or a disregard of right and wrong. She may decide to overlook it for the sake of the friendship, but she'll see it. I still can't believe that she could have been involved in a crime. But that she'd move in with a criminal, yes, that I can believe.'

There was a silence, each of us knowing what had to come next but afraid to rush in. Molly broke it. 'Your friend died,' she said gently, 'because she was in the house when the police went in to arrest some men who had carried out more than one armed robbery. Dangerous men. A young policeman, one from around here who we know and like, was with them. Quite improperly, he was left guarding the stair for donkey's ages and in the almost dark, all the time expecting a man with a sawn-off shotgun to appear at the head of the stair.'

'I see,' Alice said with quick understanding. 'So when Laura appeared instead . . .?'

'He'd pulled the trigger before he had time to think.'

Alice sighed. 'Likely I'd have done the same,' she said.

'But now,' said Keith, 'they're proposing to put the young lad on trial for manslaughter, which is not going to do Laura any good, or even her memory. And it seems that there are lies being told about it. What we're looking for is no more than the truth, about both deaths. Laura's and Mr Hatton's. Will you help?'

Alice looked at him uncertainly.

Sir Peter glanced at his watch and stood up. 'I must be going now,' he said. 'Thank you for as good a meal as I've had in a long time. I'd say a better meal if Molly wasn't here. You can trust Keith, my dear,' he told Alice. 'I've known him a long time and seen him at work. He can be a rogue about the small things, but when it comes to what matters his motives are the best. Good night.'

I saw him to the door and exchanged courtesies until he was ready to go. When I got back to the living room, Alice was already on her feet and clearing the table and Keith was getting up onto his crutches.

'It's time that we were moving too,' he said. 'Busy day tomorrow and I can think of at least one dog who'll be wondering when he's going to be fed.'

I managed to isolate him in the hall during the preparations for departure and gave him three of my uncle's carved walking-sticks, keeping the one with the goose's head for myself meantime. 'I've made up my mind,' I said. 'Would you sell these for me?'

'Of course. Give them to Deb to carry. And the walking-stick gun?'

'We'll keep that for now. It seems we may need it. For survival.'

He nodded. 'Would you like something on account?'

I would dearly have loved something on account, but I was beginning to learn something about stubborn Scottish independence. If, in effect, I borrowed from him, I would go down in his estimation. And I had come to value his opinion. I declined with thanks.

He gave me a look which seemed both amused and understanding. 'I've discussed things with Wal,' he said. 'We agreed that you should draw travelling expenses. I've told the garage to give you petrol for the Land-Rover on the firm's account. I'll tell them the same about Miss Nicholson's Mini. And if you call in at the shop, Wallace will give you a box of cartridges. In the long run, I don't think you'll lose by helping us out.'

He hopped over the threshold and then turned back. 'I'll leave you with this thought. The law doesn't allow a man to profit from his own crime. Cheerio! Bring your friend to see us on Tuesday. And Miss Nicholson, of course.'

I watched the jeep drive off with Keith's cast protruding over the tailgate, and wondered whether he could possibly mean what I thought he meant.

The writer's block was gone. I recognised the feeling. Suddenly I was almost stunned by the ideas running and clashing in my brain. I knew that the next two days were committed. By then, the flood would have dried. I fetched Alice's cases from her Mini and, after no more than a moment's hesitation, put them in the spare bedroom.

On my uncle's desk I spread sheets of typing paper and began to scribble. I could hear small sounds as Alice cleared up. I knew that I ought to have been helping her but time was precious before the momentum died. Soon the noises, the presence, the house, the whole universe were tuned out as I moved in other worlds. I had thought that Sir Peter's story would take over but, as so often before, I was surprised by what came out. When I had roughed out his plot, I found that I was jotting down other ideas, historical snippets from Keith's stories, fragments of criminology and police procedures, observations about the Scots, about life, about love; no more than seeds, any few of which might germinate and grow. But there was one sheet to which I found myself returning and adding until it had grown into an untidy docket, and this was a beginning to the story of Uncle George's death.

Bemused and drained, I came out of it at last. The study seemed totally unfamiliar and I had to concentrate to remember where I was.

Alice Nicholson, neat and prim in a quilted dressing-gown and with her face scrubbed of make-up, was relaxed on the old couch which stood against the study wall. She had been writing a letter on her knee.

'You should have gone to bed,' I said. 'I thought you'd gone up hours ago.' It was a black lie. I had quite forgotten her existence.

'I wouldn't have slept,' she said. 'Now, what do you take last thing? I didn't like to interrupt you. What you were doing was important, I could tell. Do you like a milky drink?'

'Usually.'

'I saw it in the cupboard. Do you want to come through? The milk's in the pan.'

We went to the kitchen. Boss, in his basket, greeted us with a couple of thumps of his tail. By his placidity I guessed that Alice had fed him. She saw me looking. 'I took him out,' she said. 'There's nothing more you have to do.' She put two mugs of hot drink on the table and some biscuits. It was like having a mother again.

My brain was shaking off its bedazement and I began to remember things. 'What did Keith want you to do?' I asked.

Her lips, still pink even without lipstick, turned down. 'He wants me to go and visit Hugh Ramsay in the jail and I don't know how to go about it at all.'

'Let's think about it,' I said. I put out my hand for another biscuit. She misunderstood and took hold of it. I fed myself left-handed. 'You were a schoolmate of his and a close friend of his dead mistress. That doesn't mean that he'll be willing to see you, but it entitles you to try. 'Phone the Edinburgh police in the morning and ask where he's being held. What did Keith want you to find out?'

'Anything I could get about the robbery and about the raid when Laura was killed. He said he didn't need to tell me the questions. He said that once a woman starts asking questions she doesn't stop until she knows everything down to the length of your mother's toenails.'

'He's a cynical bastard,' I said, 'but he seems to be often right.'

She gave a little grunt of agreement. 'He said that we've got almost enough facts between us and that, if we can only fill in a few bits from the viewpoint of the robbers, it'll all click together. And he said that there's a reward for the recovery of the jewels and that I could promise that a percentage of that would be held for him until his release if he could help us towards it. Isn't that illegal?'

'Probably,' I said. 'But I'll bet it's often done.'

'Not with a policeman sitting in the room listening.'

'You've been watching too much television,' I told her. 'You'll be each side of a glass screen with others in the room and a copper reading the racing page beside the door.' I was guessing, but I had to dispel her fears.

'Won't there be somebody listening in? By a microphone or something?'

'I'm sure they don't do that. Courts tend to throw out the whole case if there's any taint of evidence illegally obtained. So don't invent any more calamities. Ask to see him. If he won't see you, or if he won't tell you anything, there's ho harm done and it's not your fault. You'll have done your best. And I'll go and look at that damned farm tomorrow. Next day, we'll see Keith and tell him all about it. Then we can get down to real things. Like writing.'

She squeezed my hand and let it go. 'And I can start applying for jobs.'

That chilled me. Somehow I had already been assuming that she would be a permanency. It was not her body that I wanted but her supportiveness and the release from distractions which she could offer me.

She took my hand again as we climbed the stairs and at the top we did not let go. But, as often happened, my sexual drive seemed to have poured out with my writing. She seemed content and even a little relieved to curl up quietly against me and slide into sleep. We were both in need of comfort and ready to give it.

# ELEVEN

Alice would have been away before me in the morning if I had not thought to mention that Derek Onslow would be arriving, probably early, the next day. After that revelation, nothing would do but that she would move her few possessions back from my bedroom to her own and start making up a bed on the couch in the study.

When I pointed out that there was ample bedspace in the house, she bridled and said that she had her reputation to consider. And, no, she had no intention of camping in the study. As far as the world was concerned, she was here as housekeeper. As housekeeper, she would be entitled to a room of her own and nothing would shift her out of it. If I were a careless enough host to invite more guests than I had room for, I could choose between selfishness and making do with the shakedown myself. She then spoiled all this show of indignant virtue by pointing out that I need not actually use the couch. She repeated my words, that we had ample bedspace. Just not enough bedrooms, she added.

So I gave Boss an extra stroll, then loaded him into the Land-Rover and followed the red Mini as far as the side-road which led towards Ronnie's neat cottage. No large lorry with mud-obscured plates was awaiting us at the hump.

One stop for Ronnie, one to collect Deborah, a third to fill Sir Peter's Land-Rover with Keith's fuel, and we were off at last. Deborah, chattering as usual, sat beside me. Ronnie bounced around in the back, nursing a rifle on his knee. It looked a remarkably large calibre for the rabbits which he said were his intended quarry. Half-way to Edinburgh we overtook the red Mini, cautiously driven, and rumbled by with an exchange of waves. No other vehicle seemed to be paying us any attention.

128

Ronnie, who seemed to have an almost cartographic memory for Scottish geography, directed our course, mostly by the smaller country roads. My sense of direction, always patchy, kept telling me that we were travelling in anything but a straight line.

At one village he called on me to stop where some houses were under construction – about the fourth such place that we had passed – and he got out of the Land-Rover. I thought that he had got lost and was going to ask the way, but he walked along the cars parked at the roadside and then climbed back inside. 'Away you go,' he said. 'Straight ahead.'

I got the Land-Rover moving. 'What was that about?' I asked.

'Keith has his ideas but he said not to say. He can aye be wrong, and if he thinks he's on to somebody and you meet that somebody, he'd not want you changing colour and giving the game away.'

'I see.'

'But if either of you sees him afore I do, tell him he was right.'

After that, our route became more direct. It brought us through a village and to a farm among low hills, less well kept than Kirkton Mains and apparently deserted. Faint noises led us to a man who was hosing down a tractor in a barn and, following his directions, we tracked the farmer down in his calf-shed with his neighbour Jim Fergus. The two men were inspecting, and being inspected by, some calves. Neither group seemed much impressed by the other.

Hector Duffus looked at the three of us and picked mine out as the face which he had seen before. 'You're George's other nephew,' he said. 'I thought yon nosy devil Calder was coming.'

'He's broken his leg,' I said. To disarm him, I tapped the camera which Molly had lent me again. 'I decided to keep the date anyway. I'd like a photograph of the place where Uncle George died.'

The emotion in my voice, not wholly insincere, took the wind out of his sails. He looked for something else to object to and found it. Ronnie was carrying the rifle, bagged. 'I'll have no shooting,' Duffus said.

'There won't be any,' I promised. 'If we're left alone, the gun stays in the bag. He's only along just in case, as a bodyguard. Mr

Calder was run off the road deliberately and I don't want any accidents happening to me.'

The two farmers exchanged a glance. 'He's dreaming,' Jim Fergus said. I could smell whisky on his breath over the smell of the calves' dung. 'There's enough bad drivers in the world . . .'

'It was deliberate,' I said. 'Somebody doesn't want my uncle's death looked into.'

'There's nobody wants it looked intill,' Duffus said. 'Except yon Calder. Let sleeping dogs lie.'

'If you say so,' I said. 'But if I were a shooting man, I'd look carefully at my ammunition before I used it. There could be more than one dodgy cartridge wandering around.'

Duffus looked at me sharply but only grunted in reply. He led us outside and pointed out the small knoll, with an indication of the route which the shooting-party had taken, before seeming to lose interest and returning to discussion of his calves.

We took much the same route, following hedges from one rough patch to the next. As well as the camera I was carrying the walking-stick gun, which was surprisingly light and comfortable to walk with. It was impossible for Ronnie to cover the whole of the ground on his own, and neither Deborah nor I could see the minute signs which he could still decry. But we picked up a number of cartridges and I took photographs whenever Ronnie said that I should.

We came at last to the knoll, with a herd of angry-looking cattle – stirks, Ronnie called them – moving away before us. Boss ignored them, walking gently at my heel. A gulley carved its way up the knoll, topped on one side by a dry-stone wall. At the top, rabbit-holes spilled sandy soil. Ronnie moved confidently to a position up one side of the gulley. The turf between the gorse was cropped as short as a golf green.

'Don't tell me that you can see tracks on this,' I said.

'Where else would he stand?' Ronnie retorted contemptuously. 'Rabbits have the knack of following dead ground. Here's the one spot he could see into the bottom of it for a good twenty yards. Now, look at this heelmark.' I couldn't see a thing. 'Here's where they set down the stretcher.' He parted some tight-knit roots of grass. 'And here's where he lay. See the bloodstains?'

For the sake of peace, we said that we could see them.

Ronnie stood, pointed a finger and swung it up the gulley. 'If he was taking a rabbit, he'd kill it about . . . there. If it's not been ta'en by a fox . . . Aye, by God, there it's!'

The ground was dotted with grey stones all looking exactly like dead rabbits, but after one careful look around Ronnie led us down into the gulley and pointed to a furry shape. After so long a time it was a revolting object, little more than a skeleton and a furred shell. I had no stomach to study it closely. Cows had been up the gulley and I had to watch my feet. It was hot in the sun but out of the breeze.

Deborah had been carrying a bag of stiff canvas with a net attached, which she assured me was a game-bag. She put it down and knelt by the rabbit's corpse.

'It was shot,' she announced. 'He took the back of its head off. Jolly good shooting. Your uncle went out in style, Simon.' From the bag, she took out something which looked like a large flat pocket torch.

'What on earth have you got there?' I asked.

'Metal detector.' She switched the device on and began making passes over the ground. 'Dad got it originally when somebody bugged the house during one of his cases. He still gives the house a sweep, now and then, when something confidential's going on, although it's never happened again. Mostly, he uses it when he's dropped some small gun-part on the floor. No, I'm dashed if I can find anything.'

'Try a wee bit ahead of it,' Ronnie said. 'If it went on kicking, the way they do, it could've slipped a bittie back down the slope.'

The buzz of the instrument rose to a squawk. Deborah took a trowel from the bag and marked the place. She had me photograph the scene before getting out Keith's roll of freezer-bags and carefully bagging the corpse. She dug a lump of soil into another bag and checked that there was now no signal from the ground.

'Finished?' I asked.

She frowned, stowing away her two freezer-bags. 'It's not important,' she said, 'but Dad said to take a look around and see if the police hadn't missed any bits of gun or a cartridge or whatever. One of the hammers was still missing.'

'They could have flown far enough,' Ronnie grumbled.

131

A large and grubby van was lurching up a rough track which led to the bottom of the knoll. I stopped and watched it, thinking only that it was Hector Duffus coming to tell us not to mark his grass.

Ronnie's hand went to the buckle on his gunbag.

'Not yet,' I said. 'I promised the old cuss that there'd be no shooting and he'll kick up hell if he finds you ready for action. Wait until we see who it is.'

But before the van had stopped, a voice spoke from the brink of the gulley. 'Just hold still and nobody gets hurt. You, big feller, chuck the gun down.'

A man was leaning over the stone wall, a shotgun in his hands. It was difficult to make out details against the sun but he looked as though he meant business.

Ronnie's rifle was still in its bag.

Ronnie placed his rifle tenderly on the ground and stood back. The van stopped at the foot of the gulley, a door slid open and three men got out and climbed towards us. Each was dressed in stained working clothes and wore a stocking mask.

Surely this couldn't be happening in the open countryside? But, when I looked around, I saw that the men had chosen their ambush well. The sides of the gulley cut off the farm on one side and the village on the other. All that was to be seen was a long wedge of fields, devoid of human life, stretching away to the estuary.

They arrived, panting, below us. Most of the gulley rose in a shallow gradient, but Uncle George had killed his last rabbit – and, unwittingly, himself – where the slope was at its steepest.

'Tell Calder he'll get the girl back when he's given up any evidence he's got and told the press he was wrong,' the man at the top called out. I heard Deborah draw breath in a quick hiss. 'Keep the buggers there. I'm coming down.' His accent was rough, his voice deep.

He began to scramble over a low point of the wall where some stones had fallen out.

Ronnie's observation was more acute than mine and he was more familiar than any of us with the characteristics of old dry-stone walls. 'Get ready,' he whispered.

I was still wondering what miracle he expected our guardian angels to produce when the stones of the wall began to slide. The man on top waved frantically to recover his balance but a whole section began to go and, still clinging to his shotgun, he pitched forward and began to roll down the steep side of the gulley. Ronnie hurled himself to meet him.

I am not a man of violence but I had once, several years before, attended karate classes for a few months in the hope of filling in some details in the thriller which I was writing at the time. The nearest man was only two paces away, slightly below me and uncertain what to do. Before he could make up his mind, I administered the classic kick to the goolies and he began to roll down the gulley, clutching himself and making unhappy noises.

Deborah, relying on speed for escape, had taken off downhill like a greyhound and another man was lumbering after her. The fourth man came at me in a rush, but dodging sideways, trying to get uphill of me. I slashed at the side of his neck as he went by. He ducked and I almost broke my hand on the side of his skull. He punched me in the eye. I kicked out again, a feeble attempt this time but, in dodging, his foot slipped and he lost a yard or two down the slope.

In the struggle, I had dropped the walking-stick gun but it was beside my foot. I grabbed it up and fumbled a cartridge from my pocket into the breech. My opponent seemed not to realise that he was facing a gun and prepared for an uphill rush. While I dithered between risking my valuable asset over his head or blowing that stupid appendage clean off his shoulders at zero range, I had time for a glance around, a photographic clutch at the scene which is still frozen in my memory.

Boss was barking fit to wake the dead but seemed uncertain what else was called for. Deborah had far outstripped her pursuer but was caught up in a barbed-wire fence near the van and about forty yards away. Ronnie was down, kicked in the head, and the man with the shotgun had found his feet. Ronnie was alive only because the other's face had found a fresh cowpat and the stocking-mask was unpleasantly opaque. As I looked, he dragged it round one-handed until he could see through an unsullied area and lifted the shotgun.

Ronnie's need was greatest. It seemed to happen of its own

accord. The walking-stick gun came up and fired. I could track the shot by the flight of the rubber ferrule off the end. I must have hit him about the hands or arms. The shotgun fell, near Ronnie's hand.

I took a swipe with the stick at the man nearest me, but, to be honest, I was still afraid of damaging a valuable antique. He dodged my half-hearted swing easily but retreated a few paces. Boss made a decision and grabbed him by the leg.

I had time to reload. Deborah's pursuer had caught her at the wire and, grabbing one wrist, had pulled her off it, leaving a bright strip of her skirt fluttering on the barbs. I had no idea what the spread of the shot might be but she ducked her head suddenly and broke away. I fired at the man as he took up the chase again and he stumbled but ran on and caught her beside the van.

Boss was too soft-mouthed to hold on for long. A kick dislodged him, yelping once. The nearest man took one look and misinterpreted my struggle to reload – the second cartridge was stuck in the breech – and ran for it. Boss was going after him but I did not want to see the dog kicked again and I yelled at him to sit. Ronnie's opponent went down the gulley in great leaps, shaking blood from a hand. Ronnie picked up the shotgun, saw that the muzzles were plugged with earth and dropped it in disgust. The men converged on the van. I started running but I was too late. Deborah was hauled into the back of the van and the van was moving away faster, even over the rough track, than I could run. As with Keith's lorry, the number-plates were plastered with mud and there was no name on the side.

I looked back for Ronnie. He had vanished. Then I saw him. He had his rifle out and was running with purposeful strides out at an angle from the bottom of the gulley. He hurdled the barbed wire where Deborah had come to grief and checked in his stride to yell 'Land-Rover'.

Without knowing what was in his mind, I could only belt on towards the farm. He must mean me to follow the van. Or else to come back and pick him up. My wind was going, I had cramp and a stitch but I staggered on. Near the farmyard I crested a small rise and the view opened up. I stopped to look.

The van was on the open road, past the village and picking up speed, but it was crossing Ronnie's front where the road was only bordered by a wire fence. Ronnie had reached his objective, a vantage-point – a continuation of the rise where I was standing – about two hundred yards from the road and thrown himself down. I heard his shots, loud even in the open, and was sure that that was no rabbit rifle he was carrying. Even at that distance I saw his first shot knock a spray of rust from the van's body inches behind the front wheel. The second took out the tyre and the van swerved towards the ditch.

Puffing like an old-fashioned steam engine I dashed on into the deserted farmyard and scrambled into the Land-Rover. With shaking hand I got the key into the dash, started the engine, crashed into gear and took off, spurting towards the road and scaring the wits out of a woman with a pram.

The van had come to rest in the shade of a small group of trees. I kept my foot down and roared through the village. There was hardly a sign of people. Between houses I could see the open farmland to the left, and Ronnie hurrying towards the road. To my right, the village was backed by a long wood. I jerked the wheel, just managed to miss the back of a parked car and kept my eyes on the road.

The back of the van was open and it was empty. Another strip of bright cotton trailed out of the back. Ronnie seemed to be further on. I pulled in beside a farm gate just as Ronnie rolled over the top. He threw himself in beside me, still nursing his rifle. He was not even breathing deeply although I was still puffing.

'Couldn't make straight for the van,' he said. 'Bloody quagmire. Any sign of them?'

'Nothing.'

'Just our luck they stopped where they trees hid them. They crossed the road and ran into that wood.'

'You couldn't see whether they took Deborah with them?' I asked.

'I think not. Well, they'd not be able to get her away, not without a vehicle. They'd leave her – unless they were wanting a hostage. Drive on a bittie.'

I drove on. We came to the end of the wood, turned up a side-road and stopped. Ronnie got out and stood on the Land-Rover's bonnet.

'Not a bloody thing . . .' he said. 'Wait a minute now. There's men. Bloody miles off, but I'm sure it's they buggers, coming out of the trees. No lassie with them.'

'Shall we go after them?'

'Dinna' be daft. We can't rush around arresting folk at gunpoint. Keith may not want the fuzz brought in just yet. And the lassie's more important. If they left her, where'd she go?'

I wondered where I would have gone. 'She'd run like mad in the opposite direction,' I said.

'For a minute, maybe,' he said. 'She'd not go far. Then she'd come back to the van and wait to be picked up. Or to the farm. Let's try the van again.'

We parked beside the van for a few minutes. I was expecting a crowd to gather but, amazingly, nobody was taking any interest in our antics. There was no sign of Deborah. I could see that Ronnie was getting as anxious as I was.

'Back to the farm,' he said suddenly. 'She's maybe there.'

I drove back to the farm. There was no sign of a slim figure with a torn skirt.

'You're sure the men didn't have her with them?' I asked.

'Certain sure,' he said. 'If those was the right loons. We'll cruise the road for a bit. If we don't pick her up in another ten minutes we'll find a 'phone and call Keith. He'll ken what's to be done.'

We drove back through the village. 'Go on to the end of the woods,' Ronnie said. 'If she saw us go out that way before, she might have followed us up.'

We turned back at the end of the woods. As we approached the village again there was a tired figure trudging towards us. She seemed to have removed the remains of her skirt and to be carrying it in her hands. She was muddy to the knees, giving the impression of wearing fashion boots. I pulled up beside her.

'Thank God you're all right,' I said.

Ronnie crawled over into the back. Deborah climbed with difficulty into the passenger's seat. I saw that her hands were tied together in front of her. She shook off the remains of her skirt and tried to reach the knot with her teeth, but the knot was on the side where she could not reach.

'If you don't untie my hands straight away,' she said slowly and grittily, 'I shall ask my father to kill you.'

Ronnie passed me a knife and I cut her wrists free. I had brought along a thin golf jacket but the day was too warm for it. She pulled it off the back of the seat and spread it over her lap.

'Why did you two idiots have to drive all over the countryside and not stay put in one place?' she demanded.

'We were looking for you,' Ronnie said plaintively.

'You'd have found me a dashed sight quicker if you'd stopped still for a bit.'

'What happened?' I asked.

'I've had the worst time of my life, that's what happened.' She flounced in her seat and gave a sigh so violent that I felt it reflected from the windscreen. 'Dragged into that smelly van and my wrists tied, by men with hands like sandpaper. And we'd hardly got on to the road before a tyre went and we were into the ditch.'

'That was Ronnie shooting out a tyre,' I said. 'Could you describe them?'

'I thought it might be. I never saw any of their faces. They kept their masks on, all but the driver. He was the one who'd fallen in the shairn somewhere . . .'

'The what?' I asked.

'Dung. He couldn't get his mask off quick enough, it seemed to be bothering him far more than the blood on his hands, but his back was to me. When we stopped, he just said "Run for it", and they jumped out and ran. So I jumped out too. I used a bit of my skirt to wipe the number-plate and then got over the fence the other side. I was going to head back for the farm through the fields. But I found there was a dashed great bog in the way. And I tried to get my hands free but I couldn't. You must have gone by while I was behind the trees.'

'We went after them,' I said, 'in case they'd taken you along for a souvenir. Ronnie saw them in the distance and they hadn't bothered, so we turned back.'

She sighed again. 'Well, I got back on to the road and decided to make for the farm. There was no way I could go except through the village. I thought that if people saw that my hands were tied they'd want to call the cops and Dad might not want that and anyway my skirt was so badly torn it was useless so I took it off to

137

carry and hide my wrists. I thought that I might just look like a girl in shorts. Did I?'

Pink nylon, bordered with lace and so nearly transparent that I had been sure that her curly tuft had shown, would hardly pass for shorts but she seemed desperate for the reassurance. 'Exactly like,' I said.

She looked at me suspiciously but nodded. 'I got within sight of the farm and there was no sign of the Land-Rover,' she said. 'I knew you'd have stopped where you could see the road, so you weren't there. I turned back. There's a 'phone-box at the end of the village so I went in and called Dad, reverse charges. I gave him the number of the van and the 'phone-number of the box and he's going to call back. And you must have gone back to the farm while I was inside, because I was just ready to come out when I saw you go back the other way and I had to follow you right through the village again. And there didn't seem to be anybody much about but I could feel eyes on me like little clammy hands.'

'It's over now,' I said. 'We'd better go back and take Keith's call. And we'll have to go back to the farm. I dropped the walking-stick gun there. And Boss.'

'And my gunbag,' Ronnie said.

'And the camera,' I added.

'And Dad's metal detector and things. Only,' Deborah said, 'could you give me something to put over my head as we go through the village? I'll never be able to show my face there again.'

'Why not?' Ronnie said. 'You've shown them everything else.'

When I stopped at the 'phone-box, the phone was ringing. Keith's voice came on the line.

'We've got Deborah safe,' I said.

'Is she all right?'

'All but her pride.' I explained about Deborah's two strolls through the village. 'She says she'll never forgive us.'

'She'll get over it,' Keith said. He sounded amused. I wondered whether Molly would pass it off so lightly. 'She's just at the age to take her newfound femininity seriously. Now listen. I've been on to Munro and he's checked the number of the van through the Swansea computer. It was stolen yesterday, so there's nothing to be got from that. I take it that the men are miles away by now?'

'That's for sure,' I said.

'So there's nothing to be gained by invoking the police where you are.'

'The men have got some pellets in them,' I told him.

'So Deborah said. Which makes them easier to find later. It'll be natural enough, and much better, if you run for home now and I'll report to our police here.'

'Meaning Superintendent Munro?'

'Of course. He'll be able to smooth it over.'

'I hope so,' I said. 'I never shot anybody before.'

'Now you'll be able to write about it with knowledge,' he said. 'And Munro tells me that some of the miniatures from Haliott Castle have been turning up in Glasgow.'

We collected our gear, taking the Land-Rover right to the foot of the knoll where the van had stood. Boss was extravagantly relieved to see us return. He was limping but not, Ronnie said, seriously injured.

Now that the excitement was over, our mood was ebullient. Even Deborah came out of the sullens into injured dignity and announced that she was hungry. On the way home, I pulled up at a fish and chip shop. We teased Deborah, daring her to go in for our order. She refused, but seemed to enjoy flirting with the idea. In the end, Ronnie relented and went inside, and he stood us our belated lunch.

On the way back to Newton Lauder, we collected the photographs from Penicuik.

At Briesland House, neither Ronnie nor I lingered to face the wrath of a mother whose darling had nearly been kidnapped under our noses and had been returned minus an expensive skirt and having been seen abroad in panties which she had first been forbidden to purchase and then told never to wear outside the house. We handed over the camera, the photographs, the captured shotgun and Deborah, and fled.

I dropped Ronnie, refusing the offer of beer or food, and drove home. There was no sign of Alice. I fed Boss and settled down to work. The first rush of inspiration was over. From now on it would be slog, slog, slog, referring back always to that first outpouring of ideas. I started with the events of that day, an account which could double as a statement for the police and a record for myself, patiently typed on my uncle's old Remington, and yearned for my word processor now gathering dust in the London flat.

Soon I was engrossed. I surfaced in mid-evening, took Boss for a walk and got down to work again. I was interrupted by a call from Keith. Alice had tried to 'phone while I was out and had left a message that she was on the trail of something and would not be back to Tansy House that night.

I worked on, but the mood was broken. And I was sleepy after the day's exertions. I gave up at last. Without the comfort of work, the house seemed empty to the point of eeriness. I made a milky drink and went to bed.

Sleep was slow to come. I was anxious about Alice. She might be blundering about around people who were ready to kill or kidnap, a bondage fetishist among them. Or she might be spending the night with some former lover. And I would have hated that. She was already under my skin.

And yet my last thought before sleep came was of Deborah striding along a country road, humiliated but brave.

Derek Onslow, always as compulsively an early riser as I was a late one, arrived soon after I had breakfasted. I saw his Porsche at the roadside and found Derek on the doorstep when I returned from walking Boss – a small and sandy-haired man, his hawkish face enhanced by thick glasses.

I gave him coffee while I 'phoned Keith, who said to bring Derek over straight away.

'Have your ladies forgiven me?' I asked.

'Ronnie's here,' Keith said. 'He's taken the brunt of the attack. After all, he was supposed to be the bodyguard. And Molly's confined Deborah to barracks until she learns a little obedience and until the Scottish rural public has forgotten about seeing her knickers. You'll be quite safe.'

'Don't let them be too hard on Ronnie,' I said. 'I told him to keep the rifle in its bag.'

'He should have had more sense than to listen to you.'

Boss made it clear that he had no intention of being left behind, so we took the Land-Rover and put the Porsche in the garage. Derek, whom I had always suspected of being a countryman at heart, admired the scenery, the dog and Tansy House.

## TWELVE

There was a police car not far from the by-road to Briesland House and I spotted a constable lurking among the trees. I was careful to leave the walking-stick gun in the Land-Rover and was not surprised to find Superintendent Munro, in uniform but for his hat, sitting with Keith. They were in the garden again, making the most of the continuing sunshine between the shadows of the trees.

On the table between them were the photographs of Kirkton Mains Farm and prints of the shots I had taken the day before. I knew that Molly had a darkroom in the house and guessed that she had been busy. The captured shotgun lay, dismantled, beneath Keith's chair.

I introduced Derek and fetched more chairs from the summerhouse where I knew they were stacked.

Munro had a dark flush on his brow and I guessed that he was torn between angry embarrassment at our escapade of the day before and the hope that we would save his bacon for him. Ire triumphed for the moment. 'Just what did you mean,' he began, 'by running about the place and shooting folk? And on some other body's patch,' he added, as though that made it worse.

Keith held up a finger before I could retort. 'What were they supposed to do?' he asked. 'Find a 'phone-box and call the police, while my daughter was carried off and used as a threat to make me suppress evidence?'

Munro hesitated and was lost. 'Well, no,' he said. 'But a fine lot of smoothing-over you've left for me to do.'

'And you'll do it,' Keith said. 'Or we'll let your Constable Allerdyce go down the plug-hole.'

'I may not be needing your help, now that Mr Onslow's here.'

'Dr Onslow,' Derek said, keeping a straight face. 'And I'm not saying a word unless Simon and his friends want me to.' I knew that a recent prosecution for speeding still rankled.

Munro grunted and glared at me. 'I'll be needing a full written statement.'

'I have it here.' I took out the top copy of what I had written the previous evening. Munro held out his hand but I passed it to Keith.

'Give it to me,' Munro said sternly.

'I'll deliver it to you once Keith has seen it,' I said. 'Until then, it's confidential.'

Keith read it through and then looked up and smiled at the seething Munro. 'It'll do,' he said. 'Use of reasonable force in the circumstances.'

Munro, in his turn, read through the statement. He took his time weighing the words. 'Aye,' he said at last. 'It'll do. Almost. Write it again and leave out the bit where Mr Fiddler shoots at the van's tyre. There's been no bullet found so far, and I'd as soon not fash my colleagues with the reckless discharge of a rifle towards the public highway. We'll let them put it down to a Heaven-sent blow-out.'

'If they'll believe that,' Keith said, 'they'll believe the rest of it.'

'Likely they will.'

I put the statement back in my pocket.

A bird, which I took to be a pigeon, settled on a bare branch among the trees which ringed the garden and began to coo. Derek stretched and settled in his chair. 'What a beautiful spot you have here!' he said. 'So much peace after the racket of the city . . .'

There was a loud bang and the pigeon toppled out of the tree in a cloud of feathers. Boss rose and moved purposefully into the depths of the garden.

'Ronnie's keeping the birds off my vegetables,' Keith explained.

'He's armed and patrolling the garden,' Munro said angrily. 'It seems that my officers are not enough.'

'They're not,' Keith said. 'Not while armed men are robbing houses and trying to kidnap my daughter. Now, do you want our help or not?'

Boss came back and handed me a pigeon before resuming his

143

place under my chair. Not knowing what else to do with it, I put the dead bird on the table.

'You know that I do,' Munro said, 'and you think it funny. But I'm warning you, Mr Calder, not to push me too far.'

'And how far would that be?' Keith asked.

'That I don't know. But you've been damned near it at times,' Munro said. 'Dr Onslow, have you been told what my problem is?'

'Broadly,' Derek said. I had given him a summary in the Land-Rover.

'It is simple enough,' Munro said. 'One of my men was taken on a raid on a house where armed thieves were known to be in residence. He was left to guard the stair for a period' – he looked at Keith – 'which the officer in command timed at twenty-two minutes. During the whole of that time, he was expecting an armed man to appear at any moment. He was armed with a revolver. When, at last, a figure suddenly appeared at the head of the stairs, his revolver fired – without, he insists, any conscious intention on his own part. An innocent person died. My constable stands accused of recklessness.'

'Whereas,' Derek said, 'you believe that a nervous young man who has been nerving himself for some minutes to react quickly in his own defence if an armed man should appear would pull a trigger without conscious decision?'

'That is it in a nutshell,' Munro said. 'Can you help us?'

'I expect so,' Derek said. He sat for a few moments in thought. 'You could call me to give evidence,' he said. 'A lot of experimental work has been done recently on reaction times and signal detection thresholds, mostly in respect of radar operators and air traffic controllers – high-stress jobs in which you just must not be wrong. I could dig up plenty of data, but much of it would be over the jury's heads and the prosecution could bring rival experts to confuse them further. Better that your counsel should conduct a simple experiment with members of the jury.'

Derek paused, and the sun flashed in his spectacles. 'Best of all if he times it for the afternoon, so that the jurymen can try it again at home. It entails no more than being able to catch a coin and it goes like this.'

He arranged Munro with his elbow on the table and himself sat with his left wrist on a chairback – to produce a consistent distance, he explained. In his hand, which was above Munro's, he held a coin. Three times he let it fall from his fingers and each time Munro was quick enough to close his hand and catch it.

'Och,' Munro said, 'this is just child's play. I don't see . . .'

'You will,' Derek promised. He began to lay traps, misleading the superintendent by a small movement of his hand just before letting the coin drop. Munro caught the coin four times out of the next six. Twice the coin bounced off a fist which had already closed.

'Now,' Derek said, 'we'll tabulate some results.' He took a sheet of Keith's paper and a pencil. For what seemed an age, they persisted. The pauses before the coin dropped became longer. Derek made abstruse notations on the paper with his spare right hand. At last he drew a line on the paper and sat back. 'I think that's enough, although we can repeat with Mr Calder or with Simon if you wish. The results are quite clear. The longer the wait, the lower your score. In fact I've drawn a rough graph. At twenty-two minutes, if we extrapolated the line, your score would have been down to zero.'

Munro was scowling in his effort to follow the argument. 'But surely,' he said, 'that is not the result we want.'

'It's exactly the result you want,' Derek said. 'Remember, we're not graphing the catching of coins. What we've graphed is the incidence of your involuntary premature movements. You'd told yourself to grab, the moment I released the coin. The longer the wait the greater the nervous tension and therefore the virtual certainty, if I kept you waiting long enough, that you would close your fist the instant you saw any movement at all. I'll meet your counsel and instruct him in more detail if you wish.'

Munro scratched his bullet-shaped head while he thought about it. 'I'll speak to counsel,' he said. 'My guess is that we'll need both. Counsel having a wee game with the jurors and you backing him up with science. But I'm easier in my mind, now that we've got some kind of a defence. Until this moment, we were expecting that counsel would have to do his best with legal technicalities and a plea to the emotions. Except . . .' He stopped and looked at me. 'Did Mr Calder mention that minor items from the robbery have been turning up in Glasgow?'

I said that he had.

'Aye. This is in confidence, mind. Wee things, easily slipped intill the pouch. Miniatures and suchlike. The principal witness against my laddie was in Glasgow. There's nothing firm yet, but it's coming. We'll get him.' He stirred his loose-knit frame. 'I'd best be getting along, then.'

'Don't go yet,' Keith said quickly. 'There's more to come. Your constable may not even have a case to answer at all. And I think we can help with another case. I'd like Mr Parbitter to stay, but I think we've finished with Dr Onslow . . .'

'I could run Derek into the town and come back,' I suggested.

'I'd rather stay,' Derek said. 'If nobody minds. There's professional interest as well as mere curiosity.'

'Stay by all means,' Munro said. 'Keith, man, what are you saying?'

'I suspect,' said Keith, 'that the very first statement you made contained a serious error.'

Munro bristled.

We had been aware of the sound of a car but had tried to ignore it.

Alice Nicholson came out through the French windows, her copper hair showing lights of gold and purple in the bright sun. She looked tired and dishevelled and slightly apprehensive.

The flood of relief which I felt at her safe arrival surprised even me. My subconscious mind must have been tormented by images of what might be happening to her. I jumped to my feet and when she saw my face she blushed delicately, a very ladylike response. I had no need to tell her how glad I was to see her, and I could think of nothing else to say which could be said outside the privacy of the bedroom except to introduce her to the superintendent and to our guest.

Keith was not disposed to waste time on social courtesies. 'Did you get anything?' he asked.

I went for another chair. When I came back, Munro, the courteous Highlander, had given Alice his seat and taken mine.

'. . . fell asleep in the car,' Alice was saying. 'So I left him there. He'd been working all night, poor lad, and he was exhausted.'

'We can waken him when we're ready,' Keith said. 'Let's have your story first.'

'Have you had any breakfast?' I asked.

'I'm all right,' she said. 'They gave me something at the hospital.'

'Hospital?'

It must have come out as a yelp because she laughed at me. 'I'm not hurt,' she said. 'Not as much as you are. What happened to your poor eye?'

'Never mind his damned eye just now,' Keith said.

Alice winked at me. 'You can tell me later. For now, let me tell you. I did just as you said, found out where Hugh Ramsay was being held and went and asked to see him. They didn't make any difficulties, him being a prisoner on remand and not convicted of anything.

'And it was just the way you said it would be, glass screens and so on and nobody seemed to be listening. He looked awful. Sallow. Yellow rather than white. And he seemed to think that somebody must be listening in on a microphone . . .'

'That would be grossly illegal,' Munro said indignantly. 'Grossly.'

'I expect so,' she said. 'But he didn't want to take any chances. When he talked at all, he talked in riddles. That seemed to colour most of what he said, in fact our whole talk got a bit disjointed at times because of it.

'"So you're what wee Alice Nicholson grew up into," he said when he saw me. "What are you doing here?"

'I explained about having been friends with Laura, although he already knew about that. I said how sad and sorry I was. He was feeling it deeply, I'm in no doubt of it. But he shrugged and said that they'd known the risks they were running.'

Munro jerked upright. 'They?'

'I think so. He may have used the singular.' She looked at Keith. 'You'd said to start with the jewellery, so I said that you wanted to know what had become of it. He wanted to know why the hell he should give you any help, so I said what you told me to say.'

'I hope very much,' the superintendent said in an awful voice, 'that you are not going to tell us that you offered him a share of a

147

reward. Those rewards are strictly on the condition that the claimant did not have a hand in the robbery.'

'No,' Keith said. 'She's not going to tell us that. She might have suggested that he was undoubtedly going inside for a while and that it might be a clever idea to have an old friend on the outside with a penny or two in her bottom drawer.'

Alice failed to hide a little smile. 'That's just exactly what I told him,' she said, 'and he took the point.' The trace of a smile faded suddenly. 'He said that Laura had called me honest as the day. She may have meant it unkindly, even contemptuously, but he seemed to feel that he could trust me because of it. But he didn't know very much and he was being too careful to say much of what he did know out loud. He made it quite clear that he didn't know where the jewels were, and the only other member of the gang he could have identified was . . .'

'Laura herself?' Keith suggested.

'You knew?'

'Guessed. She had to be deeply involved. And you seemed to have your own reservations.'

Alice nodded sadly. 'They'd been close, he said, even at school and they'd stuck together. He was too fond of living it up to settle for what he could make at his job – he was quite open about that – and he'd drifted into bad company and she'd drifted with him. She could pass for a young man, in a mask and loose clothing. They were already criminals when they met up with Jack.'

'Jack?' Munro said sharply. 'Who was Jack?'

'That was the only name they ever heard for him,' Alice said. 'And he was their only contact with Henry, the highheidyin of the gang. The boss,' she added kindly, in my direction. Boss, thinking that he heard his name, thumped his tail briefly against the underside of my chair.

'Could he describe either of these nameless men?' Munro asked.

'He did try,' Alice said. 'But he's not very good with words. He only managed to say that Jack was ordinary-looking, brown hair, medium height and so on, but Henry was bigger.' Alice paused. 'He seemed really feared of Henry,' she added.

'But this is no use to me,' Munro bleated.

'Have patience,' Keith said.

'He'd only met Henry in the course of their robberies,' Alice said. 'And then Henry was mostly wearing a mask and a hat. Except just the once.'

'When he gave him a shooting lesson?' Keith said. 'And you nearly gave away his identity.'

My brain chased its tail for a moment until I remembered. 'Neil McDonald?' I said. 'He's the gang-leader?'

'That's right,' Keith said. 'From the moment I spotted a connection between him and Hugh Ramsay – which I'll explain later – I knew that he was the logical man. Plus the fact that he introduced Hugh Ramsay, not just by a false name but as his nephew. A small builder, not making money but spending it by the bucketful, renting a shoot, even his friends asking how he manages to live so well in his small way of business. Keeping the building firm as a front.'

'The hardest ones to catch,' Munro said. 'But, by the good Lord, we may have him now! Go on.'

'I wasn't all that surprised,' Alice said. 'I always believed that Mr McDonald had a devil in him. Hugh said that Henry – Mr McDonald – supplied the guns. And he was prepared to use them. It was Henry who fired the shot in Haliott Castle. He saw that Hugh had never handled one before. He brought him to Kirkton Mains Farm for a lesson because foresters were working around his own shoot and, anyway, the farm was nearer to Hugh's work. It didn't matter about Laura – when she carried a pistol it was supposed to be only for show. She wasn't expected to use it.

'When I asked Hugh about the jewels, that's when he really got nervous about being overheard. Only Laura would have known, he said. He dropped hints which I couldn't follow. There was something which he was scared to talk about at all and I still can't make out what it was. And then he said an odd thing, even odder than the rest. He said, "You might get something more from the one who used to stick pins in pigs' tails." It wasn't until I got outside that I worked out what he'd meant.'

'But did he not say anything about the shooting of Laura Kenzie?' Munro asked plaintively.

'I came round to that right at the end,' Alice said. 'I made it clear that he'd get no benefit out of the other thing if he didn't tell me the truth. He opened up at last.

'They woke in the night and heard sounds below. Laura got out

149

of bed. She said something like "It's him, he's come to get us." And she took the pistol and went to the head of the stairs. There was the sound of a shot. The pistol landed by the bedroom door. Hugh was out of bed by this time but still dopey with sleep and fear. He grabbed it and waited for "him" to come. There was noise and voices below and he realised that it was the police. He didn't want to be found with the pistol in his hand, he was afraid he'd be shot or that Laura had shot somebody and he'd be blamed, so he shoved it into the drawer and tried to hide himself.'

'Glory be to God!' Munro said. 'And will he be willing to tell this story in court?'

Alice looked at Keith.

Keith snatched a message out of her glance. 'If he did,' he said, 'what could you do for him in return?'

'You know we don't go in for plea bargaining,' Munro said.

'Not in the open,' Keith said. 'But you know it happens. All you've got him for is the robbery, which took place on your patch. So he'll come up here for committal. But there will also be the burning topic of who did the shooting at Haliott Castle. He says that Henry fired the shot. This is one of the few areas in which the law allows itself some discretion. It could argue that Hugh was guilty by association and should share the murder charge, or it could enlist Hugh's help to make certain of the conviction of the real culprit. If you were going to speak up for him and say that he'd helped the police to place the murder charge where it belonged ...'

'I could do that much,' Munro said. 'If, that is, he proves to be as convincing as you seem to expect. You think that that, plus whatever ... inducement ... you could offer ...?'

'I think so,' Alice said. 'He seemed to be hinting as much.'

Munro nodded, looking away. A bargain had been struck without quite being spoken aloud.

'So far so good,' Keith said. 'If your young man's awake, Miss Nicholson, this might be a good time for him.'

'I'll go and see,' Alice said. 'May I take him into the house for a wash?'

'For all I care,' Keith said, 'you can take him into the yard and hose him down.'

'He isn't dirty,' Alice said seriously. 'Just sleepy.'

'Ask Molly to shoot some coffee into him,' Keith said. 'And tell Deborah to bring us out some beer.'

'I would prefer coffee,' Munro said. 'If it is being made.'

'You wouldn't really prefer it,' Keith said. 'No policeman would. You just feel called on to show moral superiority over us. It's your Calvinist upbringing.'

'Oh, very well,' the superintendent said testily. 'Since you seem to regard it as a test of some sort, I will accept a beer. But I would have preferred coffee.'

'What connection?' I asked absently as Alice vanished through the French windows. Part of my mind had returned to that subject of individual identity and was wondering whether Alice's rear view looked as exquisite to others as it did to me. From Derek's expression, it did.

'H'm?' Keith said.

'What,' I asked, 'was the connection between McDonald and Hugh Ramsay? Apart from Alice seeing them together.'

'Picric acid,' Keith said. 'The lab report came this morning, by the way, and confirmed it. But I was quite sure from the moment I saw traces of yellow in the interstices of the burst gun and doubly certain when I saw the stains on your uncle's washing-up gloves. Miss Nicholson just confirmed it again when she said that Ramsay looked yellow. And look at this.' From under his papers, Keith produced a saucer with a small metallic lump in it. 'Lead shot,' he said. 'This is what you brought back from Knoweheid Farm. Welded together by the force and heat of the explosion but showing faint traces of yellow.

'Picric acid's a fairly powerful explosive, coming somewhere between TNT and blasting gelatine in the Trauzl test, and making it is well within the capabilities of a laboratory technician. Especially one like Ramsay who worked in a chemical complex where dyestuffs are made in bulk. Picric acid's a close relative to the aniline dyes, in fact it was used as a dye long before its explosive properties were discovered, and the dust and vapour easily stain the skin and hair. It used to be made in a factory over in the west, near Ardrossan, and you could recognise the workers in that part of the factory by their bright yellow colour, all but a

151

white patch around the mouth and nose where they wore their masks.'

Munro was sitting, passively drinking this in and making notes. Evidently he was used to Keith's manner and knew that it would all come together in the end. But, without abandoning my own note-taking, I was struggling to keep up. 'Ramsay made picric acid for McDonald?' I said.

'Obviously. You yourself noticed the staining of McDonald's hands. The book reminded me of a couple of interesting points. One is that picric acid is difficult to detonate in solid form, much easier as a powder. He wouldn't want yellow stain sifting out through the crimp of the cartridge. Also, it has to be kept away from metals, including lead shot, because metallic picrates are very sensitive to shock. And so the cardboard separating wad, of which you found a trimming in the waste-basket.'

Instead of catching up I was falling further behind. 'McDonald set the trap which killed my uncle?'

Munro held up his hand in a gesture of restraint. 'I suggest,' he said, 'that we avoid the use of that name for the moment. There will be others here shortly.'

Keith nodded patiently. 'Henry, then. I wanted Henry here today,' he said. 'We have so nearly all the facts that one good session with the right people present could do the trick. I 'phoned up and asked him to come and give me a price for putting a new roof on the outbuildings but he's sending a henchman. It may be that he's cagey about a confrontation, but I rather think that he isn't showing himself in public until the scars have healed.'

'What scars?'

He looked at me again as if I were stupid. 'The scars of the pellets you put into him yesterday. He would have been the man who chased and caught Deborah yesterday. She noticed, as you did, that he seemed to be using only one hand.'

I had a whole string of questions which I wanted to ask. By going to fetch another chair, I made time to consider whether any of them would earn me another pitying look and so I lost the opportunity.

Alice came out of the house, bringing with her a tray of beer and glasses and an exhausted-looking man of about her own age.

He was carrying a large mug of coffee. Alice herself seemed to have snatched enough time to freshen up. The colour was back in her cheeks.

'This is Tommy Glendoig,' she said, putting down the tray.

'Tom will do,' the man said. His voice was husky, little more than a whisper.

'May I take it,' Munro said, 'that this is the lad who sticks pins in the tails of pigs?' From his tone, he would have been prepared to believe that the pigs were in flight at the time.

When they were seated and introductions had been made, Alice said, 'Sort of. When I got out into the street, it suddenly hit me what Hugh Ramsay had meant. An incident from my schooldays came back to me. My mother used to do my hair in pigtails and one day, when class was dismissed, the boy behind me had drawing-pinned my pigtails to his desk. Miss Southern kept him in after school for a week,' she added with satisfaction.

'At first, I couldn't even remember which boy it was. So I went into a hotel with all the change I could gather and started 'phoning everybody I could remember from school. Somebody put a name to Tom Glendoig and eventually somebody else said that they'd heard that he was working as a male nurse in Edinburgh. So I started 'phoning the hospitals and Western General said that he was working there on night duty.

'By that time, the afternoon was almost gone. It was quicker to go to the hospital and catch him going on duty than to try to track him down at home. So that's what I did. Tom tried to wangle me a bed for the night but a sister with a face like a bulldog stopped him. I spent the night in the car in the hospital carpark and this morning I brought him with me. I couldn't think of the right questions, you see. I'm afraid I'm not very good at this sort of thing.'

'I think,' Munro said, 'that you must be very good at this sort of thing.'

Keith was less inclined to waste precious time in praise. 'Brilliant,' he said. 'Now, Tom, tell us your tale.'

Tom Glendoig rubbed his face. There was a faint tremor in his hand. 'I don't know that I can help much,' he said. He seemed daunted by having three men taking notes while he spoke, so I put my pen away.

153

'Everybody tells us that they can't help much,' Keith said, 'and each one of them adds something useful to our store of knowledge. Tell us about your relationship with Hugh Ramsay and Laura Kenzie.'

'All right.' But we sat in silence for a minute or more before he could bring himself to go on. 'I'd better begin,' he said at last, 'by saying that I've been through a bad patch. And that's putting it mildly. I've been through as bad a time as any fool ever gave himself. Drugs.'

As soon as he said the word I realised why his exhaustion had looked familiar. I had seen it before. Not physical withdrawal symptoms; those were over and gone. But the exhaustion, the debility and, above all, the longing, those were still to be seen.

'I was a medical student but I got into bad company and got a habit. Dropped out of university. Left home. The money ran out. I hit bottom. Absolutely bottom. Or if there's anything lower I don't want to know about it. I dare say you think you know what it's like but you can't imagine.'

'Probably not,' Derek said.

'It was when I was in the pit that Laura came across me. I was sleeping rough and wondering where to go next. There seemed to be nowhere to go but further down, yet there was nowhere further down to go. She recognised me, I don't know how, and took me home to where she was living with Hugh.

'I'm not going to pretend that they talked me round. They didn't preach. If I'd stolen to feed my habit, they wouldn't have said a word. But I'd have felt their contempt. I knew that they were on the wrong side of the law themselves although I never knew any details, and yet I'd have minded.'

'It figures,' Derek said.

'I didn't win the battle all by myself,' Tom said. 'I had help. Hugh and Laura didn't give me direct help and yet theirs was perhaps the best help of all. I don't know that I've won the battle even yet. I can only take it a day at a time. Maybe for the rest of my life I'll be a junkie who's off the habit for the moment. But by God I'm trying! When I felt safe enough, I thought it better to get a place of my own and a job, but I was always welcome to go back. Anything from a meal to a few nights. And I did, quite often. For the company and because I had a soft spot for Laura. She could

154

be hard, the way a gem is hard, but she had some of the strength I lack and I could borrow it from her.'

He paused and rubbed at his face. 'I'd have been loyal to them,' he said suddenly. 'As things were, I'd never have shopped them. But now, Laura's dead and Alice says that Hugh sent her to me. That must be true, I suppose. So I owe it to Hugh to talk.

'On the other hand, they never spoke openly in front of me. Not because they didn't trust me but out of consideration, or so I prefer to think. So I heard snatches of talk by accident and that's all. Hugh probably thinks that I heard more than I did, or that Laura talked openly to me, but she didn't. I knew that a job was brewing and then that something had gone terribly wrong. Later, I guessed that it had been the job at Haliott Castle.'

'Did you ever meet the man they called Jack?' Munro asked.

'Once.'

'Describe him to me.'

Tom shrugged. 'There was nothing very special about him. About my height but perhaps a bit heavier. Not much neck.'

'Hair?' Munro asked desperately. 'Eyes?'

'He wore a woollen cap. I didn't notice his eyes.'

Munro made a peculiarly Scottish sound of disgust.

'Stop worrying about Jack,' Keith said to Munro. 'I told you we'd get to him in due course. Tom, we can't expect you to remember snatches of conversation heard out of context. I think it's time that we began to build up the story and tried to fill in the gaps with your help.'

'Go ahead,' Tom said. 'I'm not on duty tonight, so I've time. I'll try to stay awake.'

'Do. Now,' Keith said, 'we'll start from the robbery. Three weeks ago tomorrow. We'll call that Day One. Did you visit the Edinburgh house around that time?'

'Yes, often,' Tom said. 'I was afraid to be alone and bored. I could have backslid. I was safer in company. I remember . . .'

'Yes?' Keith said.

'It's funny how things come back to you. I'd seen the two of them psyching themselves up before other robberies and they'd been keyed up, exhilarated. I think the excitement meant as much to them as the money. But that time was different. Remember, I'd known them both since schooldays and I could read them. They were nerving themselves for something different.'

He fell silent.

'May I?' Derek said.

Keith looked at him in surprise. Psychologists have the knack of observing in silence. Derek had sat so quietly that we tended to forget that he was there.

'Go ahead.'

'Tom,' Derek said. 'You say that they were nerving themselves for something different. What sort of different?'

Tom shrugged.

'You could read them,' Derek persisted. 'And you've been a medical student. So think. If they were building themselves up for a more dramatic exercise in the old routine, they'd show their usual reactions but with extra adrenalin. Pallor around the nose and mouth. Sweating, perhaps.'

'This was different,' Tom said. 'They were showing anxiety, which they'd never shown before.'

'I didn't want to lead you by the nose,' Derek said, 'but I think I'll have to. I'd have to be stupid,' he said to Keith, 'not to see what this is about. You want to know about the jewels. You suspect a row over the share-out.'

'The whole sequence makes no sense any other way,' Keith said.

Derek nodded and returned his attention to Tom. 'Was it as if they were hyping themselves up to rebel against an authority figure? Such as the gang leader?'

Tom was rocking back and forth in the stress of thought and memory. 'You could be right,' he said. 'I think you are. I remember Hugh at school, when he was determined to defy his father. He was always at loggerheads with his family. He used to have just the same expression, tight-lipped and wide-eyed. And . . . ' His voice tailed away.

'Something else bears that out, doesn't it?' Derek said.

'It might – or it might be nothing to do with anything. I'll tell you and you can make what you like of it. Weeks before, just after the time I met Jack, I was in the kitchen and I could hear Laura and Hugh through the wall. I couldn't hear any words until Hugh raised his voice and said, "I'll bet he got more than that."'

Munro pursed his lips in a silent whistle. 'It's not enough to

156

stand up in court on its own,' he said, 'but there's arising a strong presumption of a quarrel over the share-out.'

'There's more to come,' Keith said. 'Did you see them, Tom, after the Haliott Castle robbery?'

'The next day,' Tom said. 'They were subdued.'

'Guilty?' Derek said. 'Or afraid of retribution?'

'I'd say . . . both. And quarrelsome with each other, which was unusual. They were usually close and loving, especially after a successful venture. It seemed to heighten their sexual awareness of each other. You'll have to forgive me,' he added to Alice.

She lowered her eyelids modestly. 'I'm not still eight years old,' she said.

'Did you hear anything said?' Keith asked.

'Lots, obviously. But nothing meaningful. Except that one sentence stuck in my mind. Again, I wasn't meant to hear it. Hugh said, angrily, "If you had to do it, at least you could have done it right."'

'"If you had to do it,"' Munro repeated, '"at least you could have done it right." That could mean anything. It could refer to the Haliott Castle shooting.'

'Hardly,' Keith said. 'A shot was fired. A man died. What would have been "doing it right"?'

'It could have referred to slicing a loaf of bread,' Munro said.

'But I'll give you a hypothesis,' Keith said. 'What they call a "scenario". Then I'll show you evidence to fit.

'Laura and Hugh had decided that Henry – that's how they knew him and we'll go on calling him by that name – that Henry was cheating them. They went through with the Haliott Castle robbery. But when the gang was about to split up, one of them refused to hand over the haul and said to Henry, "This time, it's our turn to go to the fence with it and we'll give you your cut when we're good and ready." Henry did not like that at all, but guns were out and he had no option but to submit for the moment. Tempers were flaring. As he prepared to drive off, perhaps he made some threat. It was the last straw. Laura shot him. But it was only a flesh wound or a nicked collarbone. Perhaps the car was already moving.'

'But this is the rankest of guesswork,' Munro protested. 'Where is this evidence?'

'The words which Tom overheard,' Keith said. 'Plus the fact that he – Henry – had to cry off the rabbit-shoot and has been going around with his arm in a sling, chauffeured by one of his building workers, ever since. And I had Ronnie take a look at his car yesterday, outside a building site.' He raised his voice. 'Are you listening, Ronnie? What did you see?'

Ronnie emerged from the bushes, a shotgun over his arm. 'A nearly new car with brand-new seat-covers and a piece of tape on the dash which had a dimple as if it was covering a bullet-hole.'

'Seat covers to hide a bloodstain,' Keith said. 'Go and take a look, Munro. Then, if you're still in doubt, get a doctor to look at his shoulder.'

Munro looked around at our faces. Alice's was hidden in a handkerchief. Sitting beside me, she was crying quietly for the innocence of her friend. I put my hand on her arm but she turned away.

'Assume that you're right,' Munro said. 'If you are, we can prove it, one way or the other, when we get our hands on Mr . . . Henry. But, for the moment, assume it. What next?'

Keith looked down at his wad of notes, which was beginning to resemble a scribbled-on cabbage. Before he could find his place, Tom Glendoig made a hesitant sound in his throat.

'You've remembered some more?' Keith asked.

'That day,' Tom said. 'Day Two, I suppose you're calling it. Hugh went off to work as usual, although he was yawning his head off. He must have been up half the night. I'd been on night duty myself. I settled down to catch up with my sleep on the couch. Laura went up to her bed.

'This is what I've remembered. I was woken, not much later, by the sound of the 'phone. It had no significance at the time, but after what you've said . . . I heard the bell, but I'd been dreaming about a fire and I thought it was part of the dream. Then I came to the surface. Laura was on the 'phone. She was saying things like "Are you sure?" and "He can't be". Then she listened for a long while until, just as I was drifting off again, she said, "All right, if you insist, but I think you're getting steamed up for nothing. He isn't Superman." I think those were the words. I was half-asleep, remember.

'I woke up suddenly, a few hours later. There was a note on the

158

table from Laura, saying that she'd had to go out. If I was hungry, help myself.'

'Alice,' I said. She looked up, tear-stained but in control again. 'Alice, was that the day that Laura made the first of her two visits in quick succession?'

Alice dabbed at her eyes. At the same time a smile began to show, like the first flower of spring. 'You'll be thinking that I'm always in tears,' she said. 'But I'm not. It's been a bad time but it's over. Thursday of the week before last? Yes, it was. You think she brought the Haliott Castle jewellery out to hide it around Kirkton Mains Farm?'

'It makes sense, doesn't it? Doesn't it?' I looked at Keith, thinking that I might have put my foot in it again.

He relieved me by nodding. 'Of course it does,' he said. 'They'd hung on to the jewellery and sent Henry off with a bullet in him. But instead of obliging them by turning up his toes, Henry was well enough to be out and about next day, bandaged up no doubt, chauffeur-driven for sure and probably only keeping his most vital appointments, but showing the world that there was nothing wrong with him except a fall. Hugh must have seen him on the road or got news of him. He expected Henry to come after his revenge and his rewards. He 'phoned Laura and told her to stow the jewels away where Henry couldn't find them and to stay out of harm's way. So where else would Laura go?

'Then, two days later, Laura came back for the jewels. Henry had steered clear and, at a guess, Hugh had made his own arrangements for fencing them. But, wherever she'd put them, it was in something that went through to Tansy House with George Hatton in his hamper and she didn't manage to recover it.

'She returned to Edinburgh that night and confessed failure. But she never told Hugh where they were. No doubt they had started sleeping with a pistol handy, in case Henry or his agents paid them a call. But Henry had decided that the jewels had gone beyond his reach. He settled for revenge. He shopped the pair of them. Laura heard noises in the night, took the pistol and went to the head of the stairs, and was shot by a nervous policeman.

'Her last word was "Basket". She was trying to tell Hugh where the jewels were. Then she died.'

159

I shivered. I think that we each did so. It was the thought of the girl, a second away from death, struggling to rid herself of her secret.

A long silence was broken by Molly's arrival through the French windows. She was wheeling a tea-trolley laden with a large coffee-pot, rolls, pâté and assorted extras. She went back and emerged with a deckchair. 'Lunch,' she said. 'Have I missed much?'

'Almost everything,' Keith said. Seeing her comically indignant expression, he took pity. 'I'll bring you up to date later.'

'But I don't understand,' Alice said. 'Where are the jewels?'

Keith smiled happily. 'I'll go and get them,' he said.

Molly got up out of her deckchair. 'I'll go,' she said. 'You're supposed to be sitting. Tell me where.'

'This is something I want to do myself,' Keith said. He went into the house, moving easily on his crutches.

'Show-off,' said his wife. She filled a roll and began to munch, quite content to wait.

Keith was back in a few minutes, dismay written large on his face. 'I could have sworn,' he said dismally. 'I could have gone before Sheriff Blasted Dougall and bloody sworn on a stack of Bibles that I knew exactly where they were. Sod it!'

Ronnie emerged again from the bushes, filled a plate and a mug without putting down his shotgun and retired to his solitary patrol. Keith ignored all questions and comforted himself with food, coffee and more beer, in a silence broken only by grunts and an unnecessary grinding of teeth, before he could rid himself of his chagrin and begin his explanation.

'It fitted together so beautifully,' he said. He was beginning to laugh at himself. 'From what you said,' he told Alice, 'I thought that Laura must have hidden the stuff in a box of cartridges in Mr Hatton's steel cupboard. You said that she was determined to help him when he decided to transfer some boxes of cartridges into his hamper, but that he insisted on doing it himself. It would have explained the loose cartridges in the Edinburgh house.'

'Those do not really need explanation,' Munro said. 'A shotgun was carried on the raid.'

160

'Maybe I'm trying to be too tidy,' Keith admitted. 'What size shot was in those cartridges in Edinburgh?'

'Large shot,' Munro said. 'BB.'

'Then they didn't come out of a box in Mr Hatton's cupboard to make room for the jewels. Wrong again.' Keith screwed one fist into his other palm. 'And yet I can't be far off the truth. Think about it. The next day, Sunday, Day Five, Mr Hatton and Mrs Grant went out. On their return, Boss was behaving oddly. She thought that somebody might have been in the house. We know, and all his acquaintances knew, that Mr Hatton habitually left a key under a stone by the front door of Tansy House. Boss may have felt guilty, either about chasing away his owner's friends or about not chasing them away. Later, when it gets around that Simon is going to spend the night at Knoweheid Farm, Tansy House is entered again and the daily woman blunders in on them and gets tied up for the day.

'But I was sure that one of George Hatton's cartridges had been doctored. It might have made sense to doctor one or more in each box, if Mr Hatton's cartridge-belt was in the Land-Rover and out of their reach. Otherwise, he might not have started on one particular box for a donkey's age. So, as a precaution, I carried off the boxes of cartridges. And so, when Mrs Beattie had her encounter with the men, the boxes of cartridges were already out of the house. That's what I thought. But that's all that they are, boxes of cartridges. Not a jewel among them. Damn it to hell!' he finished.

'Cheer up,' Molly said. 'You've been wrong before.'

'Only once. That's the time I thought I was wrong and I wasn't.' Keith laughed at his own, not very original, joke and I guessed that he was feeling better.

Something had nagged at me during Keith's summary of the timetable. 'There's something not quite right,' I said. 'Tansy House was first entered on Day Five. That's the day after the jewels arrived there, which seems extraordinarily quick when you remember that Laura was dead and Hugh under arrest. Two days later my uncle was killed and the house lay empty for a week. Four days after I move in, the house is entered again. Why wait for almost a fortnight between visits? And why lay a trap for my uncle at all? They didn't have to kill him. They could have walked in with guns, or waited for him to go back to Kirkton Mains Farm.'

'That's right,' Keith said. He relapsed into gloom.

A car ground up the drive to the front door. The doorbell sounded. Deborah came to the French windows. 'Mum, the man from the builders is here.' She caught my eye, blushed and retreated.

Molly got up, sighing. 'It's like trying to follow a play on the telly,' she said, 'and being called to the 'phone every few minutes. But I'll have to go. That roof's going to fall in one of these days.' She picked up the dead pigeon and went into the house.

Alice watched her out of sight and then turned to Keith. 'I've got an idea,' she said. 'May I use a 'phone?'

'Just inside the windows on the left.'

Alice followed Molly into the house. We waited. Munro said that he would have to be going, but he sat there. We could hear Alice's voice, faintly. From her tone, she was speaking to somebody she knew well. She came back after ten minutes and lowered herself tidily onto her chair.

'You look like the cat that swallowed the canary,' Keith said. 'Or possibly the other way around. What have you got for us?'

'I was wondering,' Alice said, 'how Mr – er – Henry knew, or thought he knew, where to look for the jewels. The only other person who knew about Laura coming through and hanging around while Mr Hatton was going away was Wally, the farm foreman. He got quite pally with you-know-who while the new silo was being put up.

'So I 'phoned Wally and I was right. Henry 'phoned him a week ago about a small building job. That was the day Simon first arrived at Tansy House. He said all the usual things about Mr Hatton and then he pulled the talk round to Laura. Henry had never met Laura at the farm – he was a weekend visitor and she came on weekdays – but he knew that she visited me. Henry said how sad her death was and how sad I must be and he asked when was the last time Wally had seen her. With a little prompting he got Wally to tell him all about it.'

Keith was nodding like one of those dogs in the back windows of cars.

'A car drove past that same night,' I said. 'I thought that it was going to stop, but it accelerated away as soon as the driver saw lights on in the house. But does knowing how he knew take us any further?' I asked.

'At least,' Keith said, 'it tells us something. He'd no reason to believe that the stuff was at Tansy House until after you'd moved in. So the visit on the Sunday, almost two weeks earlier, was with the sole purpose of laying the trap which killed George Hatton.

'But why? For God's sake why? We know that he was short of money. He'd lost touch with the proceeds of the last robbery. What good did George Hatton's death do him? There must have been some back-up plan we don't know about.'

We sat in depressed silence, so near and yet so far.

'Occam's razor,' I said suddenly.

'Who's Occam?' Keith asked. He started to hunt back through his notes.

'You won't find him in there,' I said. 'He was a fourteenth-century philosopher. Boiled down, what he said was to the effect of "If you can explain something without including anything else, forget about the anything else." In this case, we have a complete explanation of the movement of the jewels.'

'Except that we don't know where they are,' Keith said.

'Apart from that small detail,' I said, 'we have a complete explanation. Assume that they found the jewels after tying up Mrs Beattie, in the place which they left to last. The killing of my uncle is unnecessary to that explanation, so it is part of something else. It may have been done by the same group – indications are very strong that that's so. But if we exclude it from your theory of the search for the jewels, we need a separate explanation for it.'

'A back-up plan,' Keith said. 'I think that I said that a couple of minutes ago before you obscured the issue in philosophical jargon.'

'There's one thing,' Alice began tentatively.

'Anything,' Keith said. 'Tell us anything at all. Prime the pump without reference to anybody dead more than a couple of hundred years and we'll get going again.'

Alice nodded, not listening. 'This is partly from hearing things and partly from what Mr Hatton himself said. I don't mean that he went out of his way to tell me about his friends, but sometimes he'd make a comment and by the time he'd done that a dozen times he'd said quite a lot.

'Henry was desperate for money to keep the business going . . .'

'We know that,' Keith said. 'From the signs, he was keeping it going as a cover by giving it injections of capital from his other activities.'

'Henry,' Alice said again firmly, 'was desperate for money to keep the business going.' Keith was going to have to learn that interrupting her was not the way to save time. I made a note of it for my own guidance. 'And he had a chance to turn the business into a profit-maker.

'Most of the executives from the chemical complex have been commuting from as far as Edinburgh. There's a big demand for houses locally. The Planning Authority refused to re-zone any more good agricultural land for building, but they were prepared to re-zone the rough ground at the north end of the farm.'

Keith sat up and pointed his finger at me. 'That plan you showed me,' he said. 'That was the outline drawn on it.'

'It was just in the right place,' Alice said. 'Not too near the works but near enough. If somebody could buy it and put in the roads and services, the purchasers were prepared to put down umpty pounds for each quarter-acre site straight away and then employ him to build the houses as well. But Mr Hatton wouldn't sell and the Authority refused to do a compulsory purchase.'

'My cousin would sell that land,' I said. 'He told me he'd have to. He was short of capital, didn't shoot and didn't have credit with the bank.'

'And with a proposition like that, Henry could have raised all the capital he needed. It's coming together,' Keith said. 'Whatsisname was right.'

'Occam,' Derek said.

'Bless his fourteenth-century cotton socks,' Keith said. 'We have two complete motivations. But we still don't have the jewels.'

'We still don't have good hard evidence,' Munro said. 'We have one of the gang dead and she can't talk. We have one in custody who may talk but knows little. We know the identity of the third, the leader, and he may have a bullet-wound in him. But where is the fourth man, the one called Jack?'

'Henry's building workers may know a lot,' I suggested. 'It was probably two or three of them that he brought along yesterday to Knoweheid Farm.'

'The jewels would be good, hard evidence,' Keith said.

'All that you are interested in is the rewards,' Munro snapped at him. 'I want convictions. I am duly grateful for your help in the matter of the shooting of Miss Nicholson's friend, Laura Kenzie. But I want to put away the jewel thieves and whoever killed George Hatton. And I want the man called Jack.'

'You want butter and jam on both sides,' Keith snapped back, 'and no bread in the middle. Springing off from what we've given you so far, you can get evidence and find the other man. What else was in your uncle's hamper?' he asked me.

'I've been through it all twice,' I said. 'Nothing that could have held a lot of jewellery.'

'If the jewels would help . . .' Alice began. There was instant silence.

Keith opened his mouth to say something devastating. I got in first. 'Certainly they would help.'

'You seem to have misunderstood me,' she resumed. 'Perhaps I misled you. When Laura offered to put cartridges into Mr Hatton's hamper, the hamper was already in the back of the Land-Rover.'

I searched for a significance to that remark and in the end I found it. 'You mean,' I said, 'that she could have wanted to get at something else in the back of the Land-Rover? But Laura's last word was "Basket".'

'There was another basket in the Land-Rover,' Alice said. 'Mr Hatton always took Boss's basket with him. He'd already put it in.'

For once, Boss failed to react to his name. Beneath my chair, he was snoring rhythmically. Keith, on the other hand, reacted strongly. He gripped the arms of his chair. 'For God's sake!' he said. 'Let's all get over to Tansy House before the stuff walks again.'

'No need,' I said. 'His basket's in the back of the Land-Rover. It's the only way I can get him to stay in the back. I'll fetch it.'

'Go,' Keith said. 'Go. Go.'

I walked to the Land-Rover. A car was parked close to its tail, which made the extraction of the dog-basket difficult. But it was only a basket with a single, fat cushion. I took the cushion. I could feel foreign bodies inside it and my spirits rose. I would have loved to search for the jewels, to return to the table a comic figure, sparkling in the sun with necklaces and tiaras and rings on my fingers, but Munro, the cautious policeman, had followed me and was watching from the corner of the house.

I carried the cushion back to the table. Tom Glendoig had lowered himself to the grass and was sound asleep, but all other eyes were on it.

'Who's going to have the honour?' I asked.

'Take something and pass it on,' Keith said. 'We'll all have a turn. If there's anything there,' he added. He had learned not to count his chickens aloud.

The cushion was a strong bag with a drawstring at one corner and filled with polystyrene pellets. I opened the neck, rummaged inside. Anything heavy would have settled to the far end. My fingers found something hard and scratchy. I came out with a necklace which blazed in the sunshine. I passed the bag to Munro.

The table was covered with papers and dirty plates and mugs and glasses. I could not see anywhere appropriate for such a treasure. And then I realised that I would have looked ridiculous in such trappings but that Alice . . . I leaned forward and put the necklace around her neck. Even over a simple summer dress the jewels turned her into a princess.

Munro came up with a bracelet, a delicate thing of golden filigree set with rubies. He passed it to me and I put it on Alice's wrist. By the time the bag had been round twice, she was laden with gems, dazzling to behold, still a princess but stepped straight from an Aztec temple into the present.

Keith tightened the drawstring. 'There could still be a ring or two in here,' he said. 'We'll pour it all out onto a table shortly. Meantime, we'd better make an inventory.'

We had made a start to listing the jewels when a car door slammed. Keith paused in the act of writing. 'Good God!' he said. 'Why does everybody choose today? Are we holding a *ceilidh*?'

My cousin Alec came round the corner of the house. He started talking as soon as he saw Alice. 'I looked for you at Tansy House but there was nobody there,' he said. 'I've brought you a cheque but . . .' his pace slowed and he came to an amazed halt a few yards off, '. . . you don't seem to need it.'

Alice smiled down at her pagan finery. 'I don't think I'll get to wear it for long,' she said.

There was a rumble under my chair and Boss began to emerge. I caught him by the collar and he nearly pulled me out of my chair. The hairs along his back had risen and his growl was terrible to hear. And suddenly I began to remember things. Alec as the main beneficiary. Alec stood as much to gain from the sale of land as Henry. Offering me a bed at Kirkton Mains Farm when I could easily have ridden home. Keith's words. The fourth man. Jack. The man who had kicked Boss yesterday at Knoweheid Farm.

I nearly shouted out an accusation. But the silhouette of the man who had kicked Boss had differed in some important detail which I had forgotten and I hesitated for a God-given moment. And it came home to me that Alec was no Jungian egoist, seeing all people outwith his own bubble of personal identity as objects and of no importance. I had not known him for long, yet I was sure that he cared about people. And in that moment, even while the suspicion was ebbing and flowing in me, I realised that Boss was not looking at Alec but away to my right, towards the house.

'Keith,' said Molly's voice, 'the man from the builders wants a word with you.'

Ian Yates followed her out through the French windows. His smile vanished as he took in the scene. Boss pulling and growling. Alice strung with jewels like a sheikh's favourite concubine. My face as I recognised the silhouette with the squashed-down head. The man who had blacked my eye at Knoweheid Farm.

He produced a small automatic pistol from under his armpit and put it against Molly's ear. His eyes were slits and he was showing his canine teeth. 'Please don't get up,' he said politely and then, less politely, to Alec: 'You. Cunt-lugs. Sit down.'

# THIRTEEN

Keith had to twist his neck round. His eyes widened when he saw the pistol at Molly's head but he kept calm. 'Who the hell's this?' he asked.

'Meet Ian Yates,' I said. 'Neil McDonald's right-hand man. Alias Jack.'

'Jack? You're sure?' Munro asked in a high voice.

'Almost.' I looked at Keith. 'The matches you were studying at Tansy House. Had one of them been sharpened?'

'Yes. I brought it away.'

'It'll have saliva on it,' I said. 'Maybe not enough for genetic fingerprinting, but saliva can often be typed. I saw this nerk picking his teeth with a sharpened match after the funeral. And he heard Alec inviting me to spend the night at the farm.' Yates was not showing any signs of damage. In retrospect I was sure that one of our attackers at the farm had had the same short-necked silhouette, but now I wondered whether my memory was at fault. Perhaps he was the man whom I had kicked in the wedding tackle. I decided that I would not be well advised to enquire.

Yates had spent the few seconds in thought and, as his face went from triumph to dismay, it was evident that the exposure of his identity had rocked his world. It is one thing to be a successful criminal behind a mask; another to face the world with your crimes exposed. He had broken out in sudden sweat and his mouth was twitching. 'That's enough talking,' he barked. 'So you know. And you found the stuff. And a very nice way to carry it around, too. You.' He jerked his head at Alice. 'Come here. If anybody else moves, one of the wifies gets it.'

'Don't,' I whispered, but Alice got up and moved shakily

towards him. Yates transferred the pistol to her head and gave Molly a push with the other hand. 'Go and sit,' he said.

Ronnie and Munro's constables were on the alert for intruders approaching from outside the garden, not for visitors coming out of the house. Just as well, I decided. I hoped that Ronnie was not drinking it all in from among the bushes and planning his own counterattack. Alice's life was too precious. My knees were shaking and my brain seemed to have slipped out of gear.

Yates had arrived at a plan of sorts. 'The girl comes with me,' he said. 'Any sign of a chase and she dies. Once I'm clean away, she goes free. Without all the sparklers, but unhurt. You,' he told Munro, 'throw me your radio.' His voice was in his throat, choked with nerves.

The superintendent took out his radio slowly. 'I need it if I'm going to tell my men to leave you alone,' he said.

I thought that Yates was going to lose his head but he saw the point just in time. 'See that you do,' he said. His eyes were trying to see in all directions at once.

He backed to the corner of the house, pulling Alice after him by an arm around her throat. In his excitement he might apply too much pressure. As they passed out of sight I saw him drop the pistol into his jacket pocket and grope for his car keys.

Munro and Alec and Derek were on their feet. I started to get out of my chair but Boss was still rumbling and tearing at the grass. 'Hold the dog,' I said to Keith.

'Let the man go,' Munro said urgently. 'We can pick him up later. He won't hurt the girl.'

'He might,' I said.

'He definitely might,' Derek said. 'That man's dangerous. He's gone beyond the bounds of what's rational.'

'Leave it to the professionals,' Munro said.

'I *am* a professional,' Derek said. 'For God's sake, let me give professional help.'

Munro shook his head angrily. He was speaking into his radio when, incredibly, Alice came back into view, still held by the neck. Yates had his keys in his other hand which was hovering close to his jacket pocket. 'Which of you clowns parked up against my back bumper?' he demanded. His voice was rising hysterically.

'I did,' Alec said. He began to walk. 'I'll move it.'

'Don't move. Throw them.'

Alec threw his keys. Yates grabbed with his free hand and missed. I braced myself to jump the moment he stooped. But, first, I would release the still-struggling Boss. He might buy me the time I needed.

Ronnie chose that moment to stroll into view, shotgun still in his grip. He was not looking at Yates but towards the beer and his barrels were pointed skyward, but Yates was too excited for those facts to register. He dropped the keys, pushed Alice away and grabbed for his jacket pocket.

Each of us reacted in his own way, moving or shouting. Boss gave a bark like the crack of doom. Deborah, at an upstairs window, screamed suddenly. Nothing could have been more calculated to push Yates over the edge.

There was a sharp crack. Two smoking holes appeared in Yates's jacket, a small one where the bullet had emerged and a larger hole, smouldering at the edges, where the ejection port had flamed.

The shot was echoed by a second and louder explosion as Ronnie, battered by all the noise, jumped and pulled a trigger. Twigs and leaves came pattering down from overhead.

There was a moment frozen in time. Then Yates fell down. He had shot himself in the leg.

# FOURTEEN

A week had gone by, seven days of making statements and attending committal proceedings. For two of those days, forensic scientists had been crawling around the house. Derek had exhausted his professional interest, given up and gone home. The weather had broken at last, but we were warm and dry, with a fire in the grate and darkness left outside. Tansy House was a warm and safe cocoon.

'Shouldn't you be writing?' Alice said.

I looked at her with affection. Previous women in my life had regarded my writing as the hobby of a dilettante rather than a way to earn a living, but Alice took it seriously. Her copper hair was shining and she looked young and infinitely desirable. And clean, despite a few spots of paint on her cheeks. She had made a start to redecoration.

'I don't want you to go,' I said.

'I'm only going for an interview.'

'And interviews lead to jobs. I want to have you around. For ever. Let's get married,' I heard myself saying and recognised it retrospectively for a good idea. It would also give us a spare bedroom.

She gave me a long, speculative look. I felt yet again the pull of those eyes. Then she looked away and shook her head.

'But why not?' I said. 'I thought that we had something special between us.'

'We do,' she said quickly. 'Nothing that's ever happened to me has meant so much. I wouldn't be far away. I won't go away at all if you don't want me to. But I don't think I'd want to marry you just yet. And I won't live in London.'

'You won't have to. We'll stay here.'

'Could we? But could you? What would you write about?'

'Keith's offered me the chance to write up his criminal cases,' I said. 'There's years of work there. Why won't you marry me?'

She looked at me again. 'You're fun to be with,' she said. 'I think you're probably a good lover, but I don't have enough experience to judge. Outside of bed, you're selfish; but men are aye that. And I think you'd be faithful and a good provider once you got over being so extravagant.'

I had been on the point of suggesting a holiday somewhere exotic, perhaps Mexico, as soon as my share of the reward arrived, but I put it out of my mind. 'Those are reasons for marrying me,' I said. 'What are the reasons against?'

'Only one.' She took my hand, as though to soften what she was going to say. 'I know that you're all right. Inside you, there's a nice person who doesn't often get to look outside. Your heart's in the right place, as they say. But you come over as ... supercilious. A hidden smile at anything particularly Scottish. And you get in little digs at people.'

'Everybody does that,' I protested. 'It's a facet of modern humour. Half the people I've met up here have been getting in digs at each other. And at me.'

She squeezed my hand. 'I'll try to explain,' she said. 'We Scots are like a family. And getting at each other can be forgiven inside the family. When outsiders try it, the family closes ranks. Well, the Scots have had enough of seeing their earnings milked away over the Border by absentee landlords and financiers. And of being patronised by supercilious Englishmen who don't try to understand them but treat them as a race of Harry Lauders put on the earth for their entertainment. I wouldn't want to be married to a man that was for ever putting folk's backs up. You'll never be a Scot; but when you can live among Scots without seeming alien, then I'll marry you.

'And now,' she said, 'wipe away that frown. If you don't change your mind ...'

'I won't,' I said, and I knew that it was true.

She smiled her special smile. 'Then it'll be all right in the end. Now forget all about it and come along up to bed.'

# NOTE – TO THE TECHNICALLY MINDED OR TO POTENTIAL MURDERERS

In preparing this book I consulted my usual sources, an ammunition manufacturer and an explosives company among them. Neither was able to advise me whether the yellow stain of picric acid would (or would not) have survived the explosion as described, or whether a shotgun primer would reliably detonate that explosive in powder form. Nor was I prepared to destroy a favourite shotgun in finding out.

The murder method described, therefore, comes to you without the customary guarantee.

G.H., January 1987

M
Hammond, Gerald.
Adverse report.